puck me twice

Boston Grizzlies Hockey Club
Book One

allie lasky

For everyone who thinks they're too autistic live the life they want…

You are exactly right the way you are.

boston grizzlies hockey club

Reading Order

Here is the recommended reading order for this series:

Tending Her Heart (Seb and Audrey)

Puck Me Twice (Sven and Vanessa)

Home for the Holidays (Jake and Rachel)

Body Check (Jason and Amelia)

Defenseless (Ryan and Hailey)

Power Play (Al and Riley)

Game Misconduct (Nick and Bex)

Instigator (Aidan and Ceci)

One Timer (Adam and Avery)

Delay of Game (Parker and Ivy)

one

. . .

Vanessa

"LOVE YOU," Bex says.

I roll my eyes. "Yeah, yeah, yeah, you better." Nonetheless, I get out of my chair to top off her red solo cup of white wine and hand her the last s'mores bar treat. Even though it's my favorite.

"Aw, you guys are like an old married couple," Elsy says, looking between me and my best friend.

"QPR for the win," Bex says, grinning.

A quasi-platonic relationship is the closest either of us will get to a real relationship these days. Taking my seat around the circle, I sip from my own plastic cup of wine. Our book club meets the third Thursday of the month. It's easily the highlight of my social scene. Work has been full-on the last few weeks leading up to the start of the season.

It's really freaking cool that I get to work with a professional hockey team. Like, I'm not discounting that. But it's even more awesome that I get to help the players settle into their roles here in Boston.

As the club has made several big moves gearing up for the young season, I've been helping the players and their spouses: navigating renting out their homes and finding new ones, figuring out the school systems, finding doctors and establishing care, legalities with visas and residency requirements, and all the general logistics that are involved with moving clear across the country—or more often, internationally, as players move between teams in the US and Canada and leave their club team home countries to play for the big squad.

But tonight? I'm going to sit back, relax, and hang out with my girls. I don't get to do this enough.

There are about twenty of us who regularly attend the book club meetings in the back of Sadie's downtown bookstore. I'm lucky enough to call them my friends. We vary across ages, professions, sexual orientation, socioeconomic levels, and backgrounds.

One thing we all have in common? Our love for books. Specifically, romance books.

My phone vibrates in my back pocket, and as I pull it out, Bex groans.

"No more work," she says, making a grab for my phone.

It's definitely not social, since most of my friends are here, and I don't talk to my parents more than once or twice a year, so she's not far off in her prediction.

Ducking her hand, I unlock the screen and scroll through the new message. It's the waiver wire—and this time, my team is listed.

"Trade alert," I report.

"Anyone good?"

"Not Wyatt." He plays for Philadelphia and is starting the last year of his contract.

She scoffs. "Please. My brother would tell me before he signed a new contract."

"It's a trade," I remind her. "And besides—"

"He might not have a chance before it gets leaked to the press." Bex sighs. "Yeah, yeah. Whatever. Who is it?"

"Theo Reynolds. From Vancouver."

"Don't know him." Bex shrugs. "I'll ask Wyatt if he's any good."

"He played with Mitch in the minors," Elsy says. Her best friend plays hockey, too, so she knows the lifestyle—and the lingo.

I swear, sometimes it seems like hockey has its own damn language, and even after a few years working with the club, I still don't know how to translate.

After a few more minutes of chatter, Sadie calls the group together, and we gather in to talk about this week's trope topic: second chance romances. My least favorite storyline.

"Ugh. Pass," I mutter quietly.

Not quietly enough, though, because Ceci grins at me.

"I think there's a story there," she teases.

Shaking my head, I take a sip of my wine. "College sweetheart. We were together for two years. We were talking about getting married. And then he dumped me on my twenty-first birthday. So, no, there is no possibility of a second chance happening."

"And there's been nobody since?" Arielle asks curiously. She's engaged to a long-time friend, and they're adorable together. But just because she's getting her happily ever after doesn't mean the rest of us will.

"A few one-night stands or casual flings. Nobody that would really justify a second chance. I barely gave them a first." I shrug. "Sue me, I'm picky."

"As you should be," Sadie tells me firmly. "You get to decide who you let into your heart." She winks. "And your pussy."

"Except maybe not too picky," Bex chimes in. "How long has it been since you got laid?"

She had an epic hook up with a dude last summer, and even though they went their separate ways, she still talks about it.

My cheeks heat, and I roll my eyes to cover my discomfort

at the teasing. I can deal with attention; I don't like being made fun of. Does anybody, really?

"Long enough that I need to invest in some new batteries."

Johanna grins at me. From the little I've spoken with her, I know she's a big fan of toys. It's weird that I know more about what she likes to get off than I do about her personal life, but then again, we are a romance book club... and she's not exactly shy.

None of us are, really. Even quiet Arielle is a freak in the sheets, though if her roommate Sadie is to be believed, she's not really all that quiet.

Sometimes it seems like everyone else is dabbling in more interesting sex. Everyone else is playing with kink. I've been there, done that. I'm not that interested in it. Sure, I'm more inclined to fem-dom than "traditional" male-led BDSM. But I don't like domination to begin with; I want equality and parity in bed, or at least egalitarianism.

Madison cuts in, and then Rachel pipes up, and slowly, the attention is pried away from me.

Bex glances at me over her wine cup. "You good?" she murmurs.

Rubbing at my eye, I nod. "Just a long day."

She flattens her lips into a straight line. "It'll be okay."

"Oh, I know," I tell her, even though I don't. Not for sure, at least.

"Hey, at least Robby isn't playing hockey anymore," she says with a sly grin. "There's no chance of running into that asshole anytime soon."

Knocking my plastic cup against hers, I force a smile. It feels more like a grimace.

"I'll drink to that."

After book club ends, Bex, Elsy, and I head back to our apartment across town. I'm quiet on the train. Bex keeps trying to get me to talk, but I'm not in the mood.

I'm not upset. I'm not embarrassed. I just…

Robby Andrews broke my heart. I thought we were forever. Maybe I was young, maybe I was naive. He was my first "real" grown-up boyfriend. We talked about getting married when I graduated from college. He was a year older than me, and he was planning on leaving school as soon as the team holding his rights wanted him in the league.

As it turns out, he did get called up by Toronto a few weeks later—for a pleasantly short playoff stint. If there's one thing I love, it's dunking on Toronto.

I don't hate our Original 6 rival Montreal; we have a begrudging love-hate relationship and mutual respect for each club's longevity and history.

Toronto, though? They can rot in hell.

And since moving to Boston… yeah, it's even more fun for me, now.

I don't know what Robby's up to. He got sent down to the AHL for a few seasons, and he made a few appearances in the NHL over the years for a few different teams, but not with any consistency. He's never played against Boston, and I don't deal with the minor league players very often.

It brings me great satisfaction that his career is in the toilet while mine is thriving. Maybe it's petty of me, but a part of me will always resent the time and energy I spent helping him with hockey at the expense of my lacrosse teammates and my own studies.

At the end of the day, I guess I'm grateful to him for one thing. He ended it; he didn't cheat on me, or string me along. When he was done, he got out. It could have hurt more than it did if we had let it go on any longer.

I've learned a lot in the last eight years since we broke up. I'm a whole new person.

One thing's for sure: I am never dating a hockey player again.

two

...

Sven

I LOVE MY JOB. I love my job. I love my job.

Glaring at my idiot teammates, I lift my beer to my lips and take a sip. How much longer until this excruciating torture is over?

We're on day three of a seven-day road trip. The Western Canada swing is always my least favorite because it lasts forever. There's no such thing as a "quick" jaunt to Edmonton —when the league sends us to western Alberta, we're here for several games at a time.

Being on the road is challenging enough because it sets my routines off-kilter. Being on the road for what feels like forever is worse.

I don't mind sleeping in hotels. I don't mind the late-night flights to new cities. I don't mind being surrounded by my teammates.

It's everything else.

Breakfast, lunch, pre-game dinner, and post-game meal with the team. Going out to the bar after the game. Outside of junior hockey, when that sort of team morale bullshit was mandatory, I haven't willingly participated in any of the team get-togethers or parties.

"

Maybe I'm antisocial. Maybe I'm a dick.

Or it could be that I just don't want to socialize with these numbskulls. I have to spend enough time with them on the ice and in the practice facility.

I like being on my own. By choice, I'm a loner. I thrive being alone.

So getting dragged out to the bar for the third time on day three of what feels like infinity? Kill—me—now.

Aidan MacGregor, the center on my line, gives me a side-eye.

"You could at least pretend like you want to be here," he mutters, lifting his beer.

"Why?" I'm not trying to be snarky. I'm genuinely asking.

MacGregor sighs. He's one of the few people on the team who knows that I'm autistic. It's not that I hide it; I just don't talk about it with the other dudes. I don't talk to the other guys at all if I can avoid it.

I keep my head down, take my reps, skate my hardest, and score the fucking goals. That's what I do. They're paying me six million dollars a year to put points on the scoreboard, not to smile for billboards.

For as long as I can remember, I've been the odd one out. While I don't mind the occasional drink, I don't like bars, and I outright refuse to go clubbing. A quiet night on the couch playing video games with Rupert or tinkering in the kitchen is enough for me.

Being on my own is relaxing. Spending time with a few close friends—I can tolerate that.

An extended amount of time with people who exhaust me, doing activities that exhaust me, with no chance of recalibration at the end of the day? That sounds like a stupendously stupid idea.

Too bad it's, well, my job.

Okay, so, technically, my job is to play hockey. But there are a million requirements that go along with the contract to play in the national hockey league, and while there are several I dislike, I'd rather play hockey than not play hockey, so I go along with it.

The rest of the guys are drinking and talking, having a good time. The single guys are chatting up women. Some of the married guys are, too. I don't understand that. It's against the rules. Why would you want to throw away your life for one night of meaningless sex?

Beside me, MacGregor is on his phone, texting relentlessly. He keeps tilting the screen away like he's afraid I'm trying to sneak a peek. I'm not. I don't give two shits who he's texting. He could be talking to the team owner's wife and I wouldn't care. It's none of my goddamn business.

Jenkins sits across the table, looking glum. The only reason he's allowed to drink is because we're in Canada—he's not twenty-one yet. His girlfriend is the single most annoying person on the planet. For some reason, he can't see that. Or maybe he does and he's choosing to ignore it. I don't know.

Next to him is Lewis. Goalies are fucking weird, and he's even weirder than most. Normally he's pretty chatty. Tonight, he's mellow, and that's even more unusual.

About half of the guys on the team are settled with partners, and the other half are enjoying the bachelor lifestyle. Even though, technically, yes, I'm single, that's by design. I choose not to date.

People exhaust me. The physical demands of keeping up with my job exhaust me. Everyday life exhausts me.

How do neurotypical people function? I honestly have no clue.

———

My phone rings at the ungodly hour of eight o'clock in the morning. There are only a handful of people who are allowed to call me; everyone else goes straight to voicemail.

My agent? Yeah, I'm picking up his call.

"It's the third fucking week of the season, bud," Brad barks into my ear.

"I hadn't realized." Scrubbing a hand over my face, I try to wake up a little. "What do you want?"

He snorts. "You could at least try to act like you give a shit."

"I'm talking to you. I'm giving a shit." Does he not realize that just getting through to me is a major step above everyone else? I don't even answer my parents' phone calls.

Not that they call me.

Brad sighs. "There are photos."

"Great. Of what?"

"Of you at a bar, looking pissed off and annoyed."

That… is my default expression. I've been told on multiple occasions I have "resting bitch face."

"So?"

"So there's already rumors of friction on the team."

"It's the third week. I don't even know half the guys' names yet."

Mainly because we brought in a lot of rookies this season. I know their numbers and their last names, if only because it's stitched onto the backs of their jerseys.

"Start acting like you do," Brad says. "Fix it."

"Why do I have to fix it?"

"Because otherwise, you'll be labeled a bad egg, and no team will want you. Remember, we've got to think bigger."

He hangs up without ceremony, the way I like it, and my hyperfocus starts spiraling.

Think bigger? Bigger than what?

My contract is up at the end of this season. Ideally, I'll score one more lengthy, long-term contract before my playing years start dwindling—and with it, my salary options. Twenty-seven is basically middle-aged in the hockey world.

I like Boston. In my fourth season with the team, I've settled into my life. I don't want to pick up and move.

Not again.

My apartment is nice. It's a two-bedroom townhouse in a quiet neighborhood where I can be alone and enjoy it. There's a gorgeous, custom-built chef's kitchen with countertops that actually suit my height, and space for all three of my stand mixers plus my sourdough starter, and a walk-in pantry to house all my supplies.

I've got Hildy, the little old lady who lives in a shoe, down the street. She always has a new recipe for trade or a sample to take home.

Rupert and I have a routine. Even though she's okay when I leave, I like to think she's happy when I come back. I don't know that she has many feelings aside from hunger and apathy. I understand that. My two main emotions are hunger and apathy, too.

Yeah, I know that I can find a new house in another city and build my own kitchen. Through the years, I've played on enough hockey teams to know it takes time to settle in and assimilate, but it's not impossible. Rupert would come with me. We're a mated pair. Just, you know, cross-species.

Pulling myself further out of sleep, I stand and stretch and dress and steel myself for another day with too many people. As I head down to the team room for breakfast, I see a few guys eyeing me suspiciously. Or is that my hyper paranoia?

Brad's words ring loud in my head as I fill a plate and find a seat. Usually, I sit by myself. I like sitting by myself. I can read the news on my phone—or rather, check the stats on last night's games, update my fantasy football roster, check in on Rupert's camera, scroll mindlessly through social media.

On the plane, I sit alone. On the bus, I sit alone. Everywhere I go, I'm alone. That's how I like it. That's how I want it.

Instead, I find myself looking at the empty space beside

MacGregor. He's hunched over his plate, his elbows cast out to the side as if to ward off the other guys.

Across the table are Jenkins, a second-year player, and McKittrick, the team captain and veteran who spends more time in the press box than on the ice. Lewis, who sat silently with us last night, is across the room with the other goalie. It's rare to see them apart—I wonder what was up last night.

MacGregor lifts his eyes to mine and he nods, so I take the seat beside him, careful to watch his wayward elbows.

My skin feels like it's going to crawl out of my body. I'm itchy and sweating, even though it's freaking freezing in here, and my heart is pounding like I've just tried to beat an impossible icing call.

I'm trying.

Pulling out my phone, I check on Rupert and then dig into my breakfast. It's the standard hotel fare, and it's not particularly good, but there's not much they can do about that. It's part of the routine.

After breakfast, we head to the arena. Warm up, stretching, morning skate… it's what we do. There's a familiarity to it no matter which city we're in.

On the bus, I sit by myself, but that afternoon at lunch, I find myself taking the seat beside MacGregor again. Until he complains, I'll be stuck to his fucking side like glue, and then I'll find someone new to stalk.

His brows lift. "You got the message, then?"

I shrug. "Guess so."

Hiding a smile, he shakes his head and laughs. "Cool. I'm down with that."

I can't tell if he's making fun of me, or if he thinks I'm in on the joke. I'll pretend it's the latter. I don't think he would be deliberately mean. Sometimes I wish I could understand people better.

three

. . .

Vanessa

IT'S ALWAYS nice when the team comes back home. They've been on an extended road trip to start the season, and even though I like having the training facility virtually to myself, it does get lonely when there are only a few people in the building instead of the usual hundred and fifty players and support staff.

Jacky comes back into the office talking on her phone. From the sickly saccharine tone of her voice, I know already it's a vendor. And from the look on her face, they're about two words away from being eviscerated.

I hope I'm here to watch it. Jacky is the sweetest person except when she's hangry.

A few minutes later, she pops into my cubicle eating a lobster roll.

"I need a favor," she says.

"Sure. What do you need?"

"Can you run down to the equipment room and get this signed by the new guy?" She hands me a packet of papers. "I'm on hold with the Austin hotel. They're saying there's an issue and—"

"I'll take care of it," I tell her easily. "Standard

paperwork?"

She nods. "Yeah, he came over from Seattle. Seemed nice enough." Jacky shrugs. "Cute, too."

I roll my eyes. She thinks all of the male staff is cute.

"You going to ask him out?"

Her loud laugh echoes in the office. "Yes. Definitely," she deadpans.

Even if it weren't against protocols for staff members to have interpersonal relations, the guy is still a guy, and she's married to another woman.

I mean, I get it. After being surrounded by testosterone and surging egos of the players and coaching staff all day at work and on the road, the last thing I want is to go home to another guy swinging his dick at me.

Taking the long way down to the equipment cave, I peek into the weight room and the locker room, making a note to refresh the drink cooler.

As I reach the equipment room, I glance down at the name on the front of the folder. Robert Andrews.

I stop.

My stomach sinks.

"Nessie!" A voice calls.

A chill runs up my spine.

Because that right there—that's Robby Andrews.

As in, my ex-boyfriend.

The guy who dumped me on my twenty-first birthday.

My ex.

What the hell is he doing here?

He looks—I blow out a breath because he has absolutely no right to look that fucking good. He's about six feet, and he has that broad goalie chest, and he—

He's wearing a brace on his knee. I can see it beneath the hem of his athletic shorts. He's wearing a team t-shirt, but it doesn't look like one of the standard players' t-shirts.

I look down at the paperwork again. He's not a player. He's an assistant equipment manager.

Exhaling slowly, I try to calibrate.

"What are you doing here?" I ask.

"I'm joining the team," he says with a half-smile. It falls quickly. "I mean, the equipment staff. Not the—not the team."

"I thought you were still playing."

Robby shakes his head. "Not for a few seasons. I—well, I was in the minors more than up in the league, and I busted my knee, so…"

"So now you're here."

"What are you doing here?"

"I'm the Logistics Coordinator," I tell him shortly. "I need you to sign some new hire paperwork."

"Oh, yeah. Sure." He gives me his broad smile again. It doesn't make my stomach flutter. In fact, it makes my blood boil. "Isn't it great, you and me here? It'll be like college again!"

Does he mean the part where he virtually ignored me all day until he decided it was time to get laid? Does he mean the part where he insisted his hockey was more important than my lacrosse, outright refusing to attend my matches? Does he mean—

Does he mean the part where we were talking about forever, and then three weeks later he dumped me on my birthday?

"No, it won't." My voice is cold. I'm glad it doesn't shake.

Robby's smile drops. He looks at the ground. "No, I suppose it won't," he says quietly.

"If you could just sign this paperwork…"

He takes the folder from me and moves to a nearby table. In a few quick minutes, he fills out the information I need to have on file for all employees.

Aidan MacGregor, one of the nicer guys on the team, gives

me a nod as he moves past us. "Hey, V," he says, holding out his fist for a bump.

Brushing my knuckles against his, I give him a smile. "Nice win the other night."

He got a goal in the final seconds of the game, lifting the team to four points above Calgary.

It was made sweeter by the fact he was drafted by Calgary and then traded a few seasons later, before he ever got to lace up his skates for them.

He smirks. "It was, wasn't it?"

Since he was traded here to Boston, and he's been a stalwart on the second line ever since, I guess it didn't work out too badly… for us.

With a roll of my eyes, I shake my head. "Get on the ice and get me another win, then."

"Yes, ma'am." MacGregor gives me a salute.

A few more guys make their way past us. I nod to Easton and McKittrick, smile at Jonas, and fist bump Reynolds, the new guy who came in a few weeks ago.

"So you know everyone pretty well, huh?" Robby says, scrawling his signature on the last page.

"I've worked here for a while," I say tightly.

Schwartz and Cole shuffle past us. Cole looks hungover, which—well, that wouldn't surprise me, to be honest. Lewis and Henry, the two goalies, edge through the room.

Then another guy makes his way toward the ice, and my heart stops.

Sven Larsson.

A million years ago, way before I even met Robby, I went to my friend Katie's wedding. Sven was there. He was a rookie back then, playing on the same line as the groom, and we were seated at the same table with a bunch of other single, underage people.

We…

Well, we hooked up.

It was just that once. It's never happened since.

When I joined the staff, he'd already been on the team for two seasons. I'm fairly sure he remembers me, because he goes red and stammers anytime we're in the same vicinity, but neither of us have tried to talk about it.

It was a one-night stand. It happened nine years ago. It won't happen again. That's all there is to it.

Since Robby, I've made it a personal rule not to go out with hockey players. And once I joined the staff here, fraternization with the players was severely frowned upon, the employee handbook stating multiple hoops to jump through, added to that, the explicit knowledge without them saying it – the players are worth far more than administrative staff. My employment contract has an entire section with stipulations and protocols for interoffice relationships.

Besides, it's in the past.

"Listen, Nessie," Robby says, forcing my attention back to him. "Can we talk?"

My spine goes ramrod straight. "We're talking now."

He shakes his head. "You know what I mean. Can we grab a drink sometime? Two old friends?"

"That's not a good idea."

"Come on, Nessie," he wheedles. "Just think about it."

"I don't want to."

"It's just a drink."

"No, Robby."

"Babe—"

"She said no." Sven rounds the corner, glaring at us. "Continuing to pester her after she's already rejected you doesn't seem like the best idea, now does it?"

"I can handle this," I tell him sternly.

To my surprise, stiff, stoic Sven actually grins. "I know you can."

Robby looks uncomfortable. "Nessie, it's been a long time."

"Yeah, it has." My brain starts to move at hyper speed. "I've moved on. I'm seeing someone now."

I see Sven's eyes widen with panic. He doesn't want to be here. He avoids all personal conversations—he avoids everyone, at all times.

Sven is…

My eyes trail over him. He's tall and wide, with a broad chest and strong shoulders that I sunk my teeth into almost a decade ago. He's only grown up since then, putting on a lot of muscle. I've seen him shirtless, working out in the weight room. All the guys go topless as much as they can, and he—

Well, there's a reason I slept with him.

His blonde hair is loose, falling nearly to his shoulders. His green eyes are intent on mine, and his mouth curves into a half-smirk almost naturally.

"Vanessa…" Robby sighs. "Please. I just want to talk."

I swallow.

Sven raises his eyebrows.

"I need a moment." I look over at my one-time hookup. "Can I talk to you?"

four

. . .

Sven

VANESSA STEPS TOWARD ME, reaching for my forearm. Her touch sends a lightning bolt of heat through my veins. I don't like physical touch as a general rule, but when I think back to that night nearly ten years ago… It was different with her.

It's never been the same since.

She freezes, and I take her hand in mine. Her eyes flick back to me, and I see her make up her mind.

Dragging me to a corner of the equipment cave, I angle myself so Andrews, the new guy, can't see her.

"I'm about to do something, say something, that you may not like. I know we have a… history. And I know you keep to yourself, so this just might actually work. But can you go along with this for a few minutes? Nobody else has to know except him. I just want him to understand I'm not getting back together with him."

When she told Andrews she's seeing someone, my shock was twofold: one, I haven't seen her with anyone or heard about anything, and as much as I try to stay away from it, there's a lot of gossip in this locker room. Two: my pattern recognition skills and ability to put two and two together quicker than most people made my spine tingle, even if I wasn't entirely sure why.

She wants me to be that person she's seeing. And in a twist I *didn't* see coming, my hand lands on her shoulder, surprising us both. "I'll do it. Whatever you need."

"It won't be an issue?" She arches an eyebrow.

"No?" I'm confused.

"It's not against the rules, technically. It's just a pain in the ass with the paperwork. And I don't hook up with hockey players," she says quietly. "I—we can't—"

"That won't be a problem."

Her eyebrows go up.

"Do you think he'll suddenly start telling everyone?"

Vanessa bites her lip. Her mouth is painted in a soft mauve lip stain, and it makes me want to pull her bottom lip into mine.

As a general rule, I don't like kissing… but I did enjoy kissing her that night all those years ago.

Everything with her has always been antithetical to my rules.

I shrug. "I mean, if he does, we just… pretend?"

Her eyes go big. "You'd do that?"

"It's not that big a deal," I deflect.

When she joined the team a few seasons ago, I was in a relationship. It didn't last much longer.

But by the time I was single, she had made clear to the team that she didn't fool around with players. And not because it's against the rules. It sounded like it was her personal edict. Something she just solidified.

Who am I to try to convince her to abandon her morals?

"Sven…"

The sound of my name on her lips makes me shiver. My cock reacts, constrained by the cup I'm wearing under my gear. It's not a comfortable experience.

"I respect your boundaries. It's just pretend. I don't have to like it, but it means I can't ask you out, so—"

I stop, pressing my lips together. I did not mean to say that. Fuck.

She frowns. "You want to ask me out?"

"You don't go out with hockey players," I remind her. "I'm a hockey player. That means I can't ask you out."

Vanessa stares at me. "Wow."

"What?"

"You just—you accept it at face value."

"It's a boundary. It's black and white. A line in the sand."

She shakes her head. "You're something different."

But she doesn't sound like she means different is bad. Just that different is new.

I decide I like that.

"So what does this mean?" I ask.

"Will you pretend to be my fake boyfriend? Just to get Robby off my back?"

"Yes." I'll do pretty much anything she asks. Pretend to do the thing I apparently already want? Yeah, I don't see the downside here.

"Thanks. I owe you." She shoots me a quick smile, and I reach for her hand. She flinches. "I thought you don't like physical touch."

"I don't." I lace our fingers together. "Doesn't mean I can't help you out with this."

Touching her doesn't make me feel itchy. Yeah, my heart is pounding, though it's with adrenaline instead of overstimulation. It's not an unpleasant sensation. In fact… I might be able to get used to this.

She leads me back over to Andrews, who scowls when he catches sight of our entwined hands.

Good. That's why I did it.

Well, it's one reason.

"Sven," she says, in a more gentle voice than I've heard from her in eight years. "Have you met Robby?"

"We met earlier," Andrews says stiffly, jerking his chin at me.

"Robby, Sven is my boyfriend," Vanessa says.

He narrows his eyes. "What the fuck?"

"We're together," she continues.

"Didn't he just get here?" he demands.

"This is my fifth season with Boston," I say evenly. "I don't think we've met. Did you play in the league?"

He clenches his jaw and looks away. He has the lean frame of a player, big and wide like a goalie. I'd bet dollars to donuts he languished in the minors for a few seasons before getting a lucky break as equipment staff.

Inside, my heart is hammering a thousand miles a minute, and she squeezes my hand so hard I think she might bruise the bones.

It will be worth it, though.

"I didn't know you were seeing anyone." He almost sounds sad. "Bex said—"

My face contorts into a scowl. I remember her friend Bex.

"We keep it quiet around the team. I haven't officially filed the paperwork yet, but I guess I need to do that now so we don't have to hide anymore."

"No," he says slowly, "I don't suppose you do."

There's a wistfulness in his eyes I'm not sure I understand.

Does he want her back?

I don't see why he wouldn't. She's freaking amazing.

I realize I'm still holding her hand. Squeezing lightly, I run my thumb over the back of her knuckles.

Her entire body goes tense.

She looks up at me, her light blue eyes bright. I meet her gaze again, letting myself get lost in her eyes. She's even prettier than I remember. She's wearing combat boots with her leggings, and her long blonde hair falls in soft waves from the clip at the crown of her head.

She's wearing makeup, but it looks light and natural—I can't really tell where her features start and the makeup ends, only that the effect is an overall softening of her features that draws me in. Her eyes are lined with dark liner and lashes, and her pale pink lipstick makes me think dangerous thoughts about her lips— where they've been, and where I want them to be.

Fuck. Maybe agreeing to be her boyfriend was a bad idea. Even though I've never had the experience before, I kind of want to be her boyfriend for real.

Since the night I gave her my virginity, I've been with a handful of women, but I'm not exactly Rico Suave. Most of the time, I let them pick me up, and I let them lead the show.

Not puck bunnies, though. I know better than to sleep with someone who just wants to use me for their own personal gain.

Andrews clears his throat, and Vanessa jumps back. Reluctantly, I release her hand, and she takes the packet of paperwork from him.

"Thanks. Welcome to the team," she says.

"Happy to be here," Andrews says.

But as he looks between us again, I don't think that's true —not anymore.

Coach's whistle blows on the ice. Shit, I'm late. He'll probably force me to do suicides until I puke.

"Gotta go, babe." The word feels foreign on my lips, and at the same time, so perfectly right. I dip down and kiss her cheek. "See you later."

five

. . .

Vanessa: Nine years ago

THE GUY next to me is cute, and as his teammates have pointed out multiple times, he's single. Bex, sitting beside me, was quick to offer up my own relationship status, too.

I went out on a date with the hockey player from my biology class. ONE date. That's all it was. So what if he kissed me after?

It's been six weeks and he hasn't called me, and I haven't called him, so we're just… nothing.

This guy, though… he could get it.

The man beside me is tall and broad, which makes sense if he's a hockey player. I guess I really do have a type, after all. His strong jaw and sharp cheekbones hint to Viking ancestry, and his long blond hair is loose to his shoulders, though it was tied back when we sat down an hour ago. His green eyes are sharp and clear. He had a glass of champagne at the toast and has been nursing a singular glass of red wine since.

Fuck. Is he even old enough to drink?

Technically, I'm not either, though it hasn't exactly stopped me tonight. The girls have been bringing me and Bex drinks all night, and if the bartender hasn't cottoned on, I'm not about to tattle.

Kate is a gorgeous bride, and Alex is clearly smitten. They're the first of my friends to get married. She was the lacrosse team captain last year and really took me under her wing; she was my Big Sister, mentoring me in far more than strategy.

Alex joined the NHL last spring after Michigan won the championship, and now he's playing hockey in the big leagues. He invited the entire team to the wedding.

Which I guess is how this guy is here. I don't know his name. He said it earlier, but I didn't catch it. I was too busy catching my melting panties.

His accent. Fuck, is it hot.

The DJ has played five upbeat pop songs in a row. When a new song mixes in, I set my hand on the guy's arm, and his strong forearm flexes.

Slowly, he swivels his head in my direction.

"Would you like to dance?" I ask.

He swallows, his Adam's apple bobbing, and I have the weirdest urge to lick it. Lick him.

Lick him everywhere.

Pressing my knees together, I squeeze my thighs to redirect my attention away from the pulsing between my legs. It's been a long time since I've gotten laid. Too long.

"Dance?" he asks in that panty-incinerating accent.

"Yeah. Do you want to dance?"

"With you?" His eyes go wide.

Why does he sound so surprised?

I can't deny that stings. With a huff, I cross my arms over my chest and glare at him.

"Yeah, with me."

He swallows again, and I realize the entire table has fallen silent, watching us.

"Come on, man," says one of the guys. "Just do it."

"It'll be good for you," chimes in another hockey player. "Put some hair on your chest."

"Fuck off," he mutters, scowling at his teammate. "Fine. Yes. Let's dance."

Pushing back my chair, I rise to my feet and let the crepe fabric of my skirt fall to the floor. It's a gorgeous dress; a dark plum purple halter, an exposed back, and a soft, delicate skirt that makes me feel like a ballerina. My long blonde hair is tied up into a French twist, a few strands of curls hanging free to give the style a tousled look. I look fucking hot and I know it.

I'm tall, and with my heels, I'm even taller. This guy, though? He stands about six foot three, and his dark blue three-piece suit is fucking stellar, and when he comes to stand beside me, I get the faintest whiff of crisp, clean cologne and a hint of musk that sends all my senses into overdrive.

His warm palm lands on the small of my back, and I flinch. He pulls his hand away.

The dance floor is crowded with people bopping along to the 90s jams the DJ has been blasting. I see a few people giving us curious looks as I lead him to an empty patch of the dance floor.

Shaking and shimmying to the music, I let my body loosen to the last verse of the song as he stands stiffly beside me.

He looks uncomfortable, like he'd rather be anywhere else on the fucking planet than here with me.

And normally, I'd let that bother me.

But this is just a dance, this is just one night out of my life, and if I never see him again, it's not a big deal. He's hot, sure, but it's not like I'm gonna marry the guy or anything.

The song transitions to a slower melody. Before I can think too much about it, I place my hand on his shoulder and he sets a hand on my waist.

"I've never done this before," he murmurs, pulling me close.

"Done what? Slow danced?"

His soft exhale draws me in.

"I've never held a beautiful woman in my arms and wished she could be mine."

With a scoff, I pull back. "You—"

He moves his hands to my hips, putting a polite distance between us. "You are beautiful," he says in perfect English with the crispest tinge to his words. "I know you can't be mine."

"Why not?" I look up at him.

There's a freckle on the end of his nose. I want to kiss it.

I've forgotten why this can't work.

"Because I've never been lucky enough to have my dreams come true," he says, his eyes meeting mine.

He's serious.

What the hell?

"You play in the National Hockey League. You're—you're living the dream!"

He shrugs. "Hockey was a goal. Something I could work hard to attain. Something measurable. You would be a dream, and I'd never be able to work hard enough to get you... much less keep you."

I blink at him a few times, wondering where in the actual hell this guy came from. "Again… you're in the fucking NHL. I bet you wouldn't have to work a single day for the girls throwing their panties at you." Fuck knows I'd be first in line to throw my own.

"I don't want girls," he says, with a slight sneer.

"Guys? Hey, I'm cool with that."

His fingers slide inward, meeting in the small of my back as he turns me.

"No, not guys. I don't want girls. I want a woman. One woman."

Playing coy, I run my hand through the hair at the nape of his neck. "Who? Maybe I could introduce you."

His eyes meet mine. "You."

With a forceful tug, I drag him down to my level and kiss him roughly. His soft lips collide with mine using a little too much force, and his teeth crash into mine with an uncomfortable clack.

Reeling back, I pull away.

This was a mistake. I shouldn't be doing this.

He moves his hand to my face, cupping my cheek as his eyes search mine.

Finally, blessedly, he brings his mouth to mine, gentle now as his lips brush against my own.

I'm glad we got that bad crash out of the way, because now there's nothing stopping this from being the sweetest, most perfect kiss that ever was.

I'm floating on a cloud of air, lost in a sea of possibility and wonder. My stomach jumps with butterflies, my skin feels all tingly, and I swear I'm blushing.

This guy… I don't even know his name, but I already know I'm quite smitten.

His thumb strokes my cheek, and he looks down at me. His lips part, his eyes wide.

"Wow," he breathes.

Oh, he's pressing all of my pleasure buttons.

Metaphorically, I mean. Not literally.

Although… he could.

"You want to get out of here?" I murmur.

He gulps.

I tiptoe my fingers down his sternum. "Maybe…"

"Yeah?" His voice cracks.

"We can get to know each other a little better," I whisper. My eyes flick up to his. "Clothing is optional."

six

. . .

Sven: Nine years ago

THIS WOMAN... she's, like, ten times out of my league. I'm not even in the league, I'm watching from the bleachers as everyone else competes around me. There's a reason I'm a nineteen-year-old virgin playing in the National Hockey League.

I mean, I've fooled around before. I've been set up on blind dates, and I've taken a teammate's sister to the annual hockey gala at the end of the season. There was a little bit of kissing at the Halloween party, and—

I've never been naked in the presence of a woman.

In high school, I always had more important things to worry about, like hockey. When I moved to Canada for my rookie season, I couldn't afford to let myself get distracted. And now...

Well, everyone I know already knows how to do this. I mean, I get the gist. Tab A goes into Slot B. I've seen enough videos to understand what goes where. I'm sure it feels good. I just... I don't know *how*.

Vanessa's hand in mine drags me toward the elevator bank, and as we wait, she curls herself into my body, her arm low around my waist.

Typically, I'm touch averse. I don't like physical contact, but the feeling of her warm skin on mine is making me dizzy in a good way. Her hand slides under my suit jacket to press against my abs over my vest. She nuzzles closer, her face buried in my neck, peppering light kisses along my jaw.

I have no idea what she sees in me. Is it just a score? A hockey player to check off her list?

No, she doesn't seem like a puck bunny. I've been propositioned enough at the bars to know when a woman just wants the attention. She seems like she actually wants me, regardless of what I do for a living.

Somehow, that makes me feel worse. My stomach sinks. Nobody wants me, not in that way. Nobody ever has before. I don't know why she's pretending to be interested.

The elevator dings and we step in. She presses the button for the seventh floor and then curls into me again. Her face presses into my neck, enveloping me in her light floral scent.

When the doors open on her floor, she releases me to swipe her key, and then she beckons me to follow her into her room.

It's a generic hotel room. Two double beds, one with clothes layered on top of the linens. Two suitcases — both open, messily stuffed full of clothes.

Vanessa turns to me, hands on her hips. "What's your deal, dude?"

"My deal?"

"Yeah. Are you not interested in this? You haven't tried to, like, take off my clothes or feel me up or anything."

"Do you know who I am?" I ask.

She scowls.

"Do you know my name?" I rephrase.

Vanessa squints. "Shawn? Scott? Does it matter?"

"It matters." Shaking my head, I exhale slowly. "Sven."

"Hi, Sven," she says. "I'm Vanessa. Are you going to fuck me or not?"

It's my turn to squint at her.

"Why do you want me to fuck you?"

The word is harsh and foreign on my tongue. Even though I toss around plenty of "fucks" in my everyday vernacular, using it in this context is strange and new.

She blinks at me. "Because you're gorgeous, and I want your massive Viking dick inside of me. Does it have to be anything more than that?"

This isn't how I wanted my first time to go. This isn't what I pictured. I don't want to be used.

"Can we just… slow down?" I pull at my tie, sitting on the edge of the bed.

She sits beside me, one leg propped between us. Her blue eyes are curious.

"Everything okay?" she asks.

"I—I don't do this. This isn't what I do." Running my hands over my pants, I look at her. "I don't pick up random women. I don't sleep around."

Her expression softens. "Am I coming on too strong?"

When I nod, she sighs.

"This guy—" She blows out a breath. "You don't want to hear about it."

I do, though. Scooting closer, I set my hand on her hip.

"We went out on a date. And I thought he was interested. But it's been a while and it's clear he's not, and I—I'm just a little bruised. I don't like rejection," she mutters.

"Nobody does."

She shrugs. "Well, my friend Bex made this big deal about me getting back on the horse. I need to put myself out there again. And I guess… I went too far. I overcommitted."

I give into the urge to coil one of her curls around my finger.

"I know a little about overcommitting."

She raises her brows at me, encouraging me to elaborate.

"My singular focus for the last fifteen years has been

hockey. It's the only thing that matters." I lift my shoulders. "I'm good at hyper focus. That's my jam."

Vanessa's soft smile makes my stomach hurt. "What else is your jam?"

Toeing off my shoes, I pull off my jacket and toss it on the desk chair, then settle back against the pillows of the bed. She does the same, sliding off her heels and then coming to lay opposite me, her cheek on the pillow as she gazes up at me.

"I'm really good at chess," I admit. "I was in several competitions back home."

"Finland?"

"Sweden," I correct. "I'm from a small town outside of Stockholm."

"That must be nice," she says wistfully. "I'm from Oregon, right on the border next to California."

"Tell me about it. What's it like?" I card my fingers through her hair, cupping her cheek because I just have to touch her.

Her hand comes to rest on mine, holding me to her.

"It was fine."

When I snort out a laugh, she smiles.

"It's fine," she repeats. "My parents live two towns apart, so I spent a lot of time going between their houses."

"Do you have siblings?"

She shrugs. "I mean, my parents both got married and had new kids. But they're not my siblings. They're just my parents' kids."

I don't know what to say to that.

"How do you know the bride and groom?"

"We were on the same lacrosse team at Michigan," Vanessa says. "I'll miss her next year. I have two years left."

"Jackson and I play on the same line," I contribute. He's a left winger and I'm on the right side.

We talk idly, learning about each other. She likes junk food and salad though not at the same time, hates bell peppers, is moderately obsessed with pesto sauce, and has no idea what she wants to do after she graduates.

"I've never had a one-night stand before," I admit.

"Me, either," she whispers.

Slowly, I bring my lips to hers. Her eyes flutter closed, and she exhales against me, melting into the pillows. She tastes sweet, like the champagne she was drinking earlier, and I don't know how I've lived this long without doing this.

Vanessa squirms closer, her hand on my chest. I want to put my hand somewhere—do I hold her waist again?—when she takes my hand and presses it to her chest, in the same position as hers on mine.

Her breasts are round and plush. The sensation is nothing like I've ever felt before. Twisting my wrist, I cup her and run my thumb over the pebble in the center of the swell, and she lets out a soft moan.

Her fingers tweak my nipple, and I swear my cock goes rock-hard in about two-point-seven seconds.

Moving on instinct, I pull her body into me, and I know she can feel my natural reaction to her ministrations. She grinds against my hardness. My eyes roll back in my head and I swear—

"I'd really like to suck your dick," she says, and my traitorous cock jerks against her in my suit pants. "Is that okay with you?"

With my quick, insistent nod, she smiles, her hands moving to my belt. She gets my pants open and then slides her hand into my underwear.

The first contact of her palm against my cock has me panting like there's an open goal on a power play, and I have the puck. I've never had another person's hand on my dick before.

Vanessa draws me out, squeezing her hand around the base and then stroking the shaft, sticky from the pre-cum leaking from the tip. Her tongue comes out to wet her lips, and I twitch in her grip.

Her shove on my shoulder has me rolling onto my back, and she works my pants and boxers down my hips to pull them off. I'm still wearing my waistcoat, so I unbutton that, too, and then my shirt, leaving me naked in the bed.

She's still wearing her dress.

"I want to see you," I tell her. "Can I see you?"

Her blue eyes lock on mine, her fist around my dick, stroking torturously slow, as she nods silently.

There's a clasp behind her neck. I tug at the strings, and the front of her dress falls away, leaving her bare from the waist up.

Her tits are—

A fresh dribble of pre-cum works its way out of me, and she smirks, leaning down to swipe her tongue across the head of my dick.

When I groan, she takes more of me into her mouth, sucking on the head and then drawing me inside, swallowing around my length.

Holy fucking shit.

My hips jerk automatically, pushing more of my erection into her mouth.

Her eyes fall closed, her fist tightens around the base of my cock, and she works me into her mouth until her fist meets her lips.

I think I'm dying.

My right hand never felt as good as this feels right now. Hot, wet suction around my dick, and her tongue swirls around the sensitive slit of my cockhead as her hand slowly strokes the shaft.

Fisting the sheet with one hand, I curl my fingers into my palm with the other, biting my knuckles to keep from crying out.

Her hand cups my balls, rolling them in her palm. I didn't

know they were so sensitive. My mouth falls open in a silent O, and she sucks on the sensitive vein running along the underside of my cock.

"It's okay," she murmurs. "Let it go."

She squeezes lightly on my balls, her fingers pressing on my taint, and I—

Without warning, my cock jerks, and she pulls me into her mouth just before the orgasm barrels into me. The hot, wet suction of her mouth around me is an exquisite heaven that I never want to end.

In videos, sometimes the giver swallows, and sometimes they don't. I don't know what happens in real life. But as I watch, her throat works, swallowing my load, and I swear another gush comes from my cock at the sight.

Vanessa pulls back, looking mighty pleased, and she presses a soft kiss to the tip of my dick.

"What the fuck," I manage, working to get air back into my lungs.

She looks up at me, her eyebrow quirked. "Excuse me?"

"I don't think I've ever come that hard in my life," I admit.

A pleased smile spreads across her face.

Reaching for her hand, I squeeze it. I'm not capable of much more than that right now.

Being touched on the ice doesn't bother me because it's part of the game. But off it? Mingled with the general population who have no reason to touch me? No. No thank you.

Vanessa pulls away and shucks the rest of her dress, leaving her in a tiny pair of black satin panties, and then slides up the bed to rest her head on the pillow opposite mine. Her hand lands on my chest, sticky from touching me.

I curl toward her, setting my hand on her hip and pulling her body into me. She smiles at me, her face hesitant.

Lowering my mouth to hers, I kiss her, and even though she tastes like me, I actually really like it. She softens, becoming pliant, and as I sweep my tongue into her mouth, she melts against me, half pulling me on top of her.

Her legs wrap around my waist, and I push up slightly to look at her body pressed intimately to mine. Even through her panties, I can feel the wet heat of her pressing against my spent cock, and it sends a bolt of need through me.

She pins her shoulders to the bed, pushing out her chest. "Like what you see?"

I close my palm around her breast, my thumb rubbing over her nipple, which tightens beneath my touch. "Yeah. A lot."

As I lean down, I draw her other breast into my mouth, sucking gently. Based on the way she runs her hand through my hair and pulls me closer, I'm thinking she likes this. Kissing and nibbling, I memorize the taste of her skin, salty and sweet, a flavor I will never get enough of.

Her hips tilt up into mine.

My eyes flick to hers, and as I trail a hand down her side to her waist, she nods quickly.

Sliding her panties over her hips, I'm treated to my first up close and personal look at a pussy. It looks different than in videos. It smells good, too—my mouth waters; I need to taste her.

She's waxed and hairless, her skin warm and smooth. I trail my hands up her thighs. When my skin doesn't prickle at the feeling of hers, I do it again, and I duck my head, hiding my smile in her pussy.

Vanessa lets out a soft pant, running her fingers through my hair.

"I don't know what I'm doing," I tell her honestly, trailing my finger through her wet seam. "You'll have to tell me if this is what you like."

"Oh, don't worry," she says with a confident grin. "I will."

seven

. . .

Vanessa

SVEN BRINGS a turkey pesto sandwich to my desk. He stands outside my cubicle, staring at me until I turn to face him.

"Can I help you?" I look away from my spreadsheets for a moment.

He thrusts the sandwich at me. "We need to talk."

"Now?" Jacky's in a meeting with Coach Turner—she'll be back soon.

I don't know what came over me. Why did I say it? Why did I lie to Robby?

Why did Sven play along?

"I'm sorry," I tell him. "I think we're starting off on the wrong foot. I'll go back down there, tell him it was all a misunderstanding. I can have coffee with him or whatever."

"You were together." It's a statement, not a question.

I nod. "We… right after you and I… we started dating. And then two and a half years later, we broke up. I haven't seen him since."

Sven winces. "Ouch."

Shrugging, I try to play it cool. "It's fine. I'm fine."

He snorts. "Yeah, okay. And I'm neurotypical."

Squinting at him, I try to understand. "What do you mean?"

But he shakes his head. "Do you want to get back with him?"

My stomach turns.

Do I?

No.

Not even a little bit.

The revolted expression on my face makes Sven crack a smile.

"So, until further notice, we're dating," he says quietly. "Is that going to be an issue for you? With your job?"

It is. It absolutely is. They're sticklers about protocols, especially when it comes to players, so I have to rectify it quickly, especially now that Robby thinks Sven and I are dating. Especially since Sven kissed my cheek and held my hand in the bowels of the arena around other players.

This isn't going to be easy to keep quiet now, and I have no idea if it's going to be okay. But I'm committed now. And I'm not sure how to reconcile that commitment with the knowledge that I did it, fully aware that it's against the rules.

It's like Sven scrambled all the edges of my brain.

Again.

"I'll figure it out," I say instead. "There's—it's fine."

"Are we ever going to talk about what happened?" Sven asks, cocking his head. "Or are we going to pretend it never happened for another nine years?"

I gulp. "So you do remember."

"Vividly." He presses his lips together, then looks away. "I apologize if I've made you uncomfortable."

"You haven't." I think back to when I first started with the team. "You never mentioned it, so I assumed you forgot or just didn't care."

Sven shrugs. "Neither did you. Did you forget? Did you not care?"

All I remember was that I didn't want the team to think I was trying to sleep my way to a job—or worse, use the job to launch myself into the bed of a player. I wanted to get by on my own merit. Besides, he was seeing someone when I started—I was hardly about to bring up our one-night stand when he was happily committed to another woman.

"We might have to pretend for a while," I start slowly. "We can break up in a few weeks."

"That's fine." He gestures to the sandwich. "You need to eat."

How did he know I skipped lunch today? Unwrapping the sandwich, I pick out the tomatoes ruining it before taking a hearty bite. *He remembered I love pesto.*

"You won't be able to go out with anyone else for a little while," I warn him. "As long as we're pretending…"

Sven shakes his head. "I understand what you're asking of me."

"There won't be any problems with that?" I lift my brows. "Any… other partners who may come forward?"

He snorts. "Yeah, that's not an issue."

"What, are you, like, a monk or something?"

His eyes soften. "Something like that," he admits. "I don't go out much."

"When was your last relationship?"

"When was yours?" He counters.

"I don't do relationships. I've been single for a while." I shrug. "It's what I want."

"And this won't be an issue?" He moves his finger between us. "There's nobody else who may have a contradictory history?"

"No, because it's not real." I'm matter of fact. "We're just pretending. In a few weeks, we'll break up."

He mutters something in Swedish under his breath.

I barrel forward, fabricating a story I hope is believable. "It happened over summer. We ran into each other and…" I trail off.

"Fine," Sven says crisply.

I blow out a breath. We can do this.

This is a lot. I don't know Sven, not really. We hooked up—once—nine years ago. It never went beyond that. I didn't follow his career. It's only by chance that we both work in hockey now for the same team—him still on the ice, me behind the scenes.

Fuck. I have to tell my boss about this.

"What are we doing?" I scrub at my eyes, and as they come away gritty with dark smudges, I realize I've just smeared my eye makeup. "What the fuck is today?"

To my surprise, Sven laughs, his body relaxing. "I could ask you the same thing."

"Why are you doing this? Why are you helping me?"

He shrugs. "You looked uncomfortable. I didn't like it."

"That's it?"

"That's it," he repeats.

"No ulterior motives?"

He frowns. "I didn't like the way he was talking to you."

That doesn't ease my anxiety in the slightest.

"Robby's fine. He won't hurt me. He's just—"

"He tried to make you small. He talked down to you. He made you afraid." A scowl crosses his pretty face. "I don't like it."

There's a noise behind us, and immediately Sven moves, blocking me in with his broad frame—so nobody can catch sight of me in my cubicle with him? So he can protect me again? I don't know.

He glances around. "Do we tell everyone?"

"I don't know. I've never done this before."

"That's my line," he mutters under his breath.

Glaring at him, I poke him in the chest. "I don't date hockey players, and I—"

He captures my finger, smoothly sliding my hand into his and lacing our fingers together. "I know you don't."

Patrice, the communications guru, enters the back office. He turns to look at her but doesn't disengage.

"I should go," he sighs.

Nodding, I agree, "That's probably for the best."

"Text me," he says, squeezing my hand. "We'll figure this out."

———

Jacky calls me into her office around three. Blowing out a breath, I grab the paperwork and approach.

"We need to talk," she says.

My stomach drops. "Okay."

"I'm sure you've noticed some things are... different around here."

My eyebrows go up. "Uh... yeah?" I mean, I haven't, but I can pretend.

Her hand falls to her belly. "I'm not going to be able to travel for much longer."

"Is everything okay?"

Jacky shakes her head. "It's high-risk, and I'm not talking about it because it freaks me the fuck out, but my doctor is this close to grounding me. So I won't be able to travel with the team for much longer."

I knew she and Jo were trying for another baby in theory. I wasn't privy to all of the sensitive details. I don't need to know until I need to know.

I guess I need to know now.

"So you want me to travel with the team?"

Until now, I've handled everything from the ground. I don't travel. Every once in a while, I can request to attend an away game, but it's still work, and it's not exactly restful. Besides, I don't want my life to revolve around work.

"You and Scott will split the games," Jacky continues. "You have seniority so you get to pick your preferred trips, but it'll be as close to 50/50 coverage as we can get it."

I swallow. Road trips. That's not the end of the world. I could be getting fired. I'm glad it's not that.

"Whatever you need," I tell my boss quickly.

Jacky rubs her fingers together in the universal sign for money.

Right. She can't volunteer that information. I have to ask for it.

"Is there additional compensation for the added responsibilities?"

She smiles. "Yes, I'm authorized to double the per diem and offer a five percent permanent total salary increase."

"Five percent?" That's almost nothing. It'll barely make a difference after they take out the taxes.

"Your position is salaried, not hourly, and does not account for overtime." She winces. "Since this is a temporary adjustment of duties and not a change in job function, the budget is constrained. All of your travel expenses are covered, of course. And your meals while on the trip. This salary increase will not be factored into your cost of living adjustment and performance-based increases."

With a sigh, I roll the idea around in my head. It's not that bad of a deal. It could be a lot worse.

My eyes fall to the paper in my hands. The one I printed and filled out with mostly lies before I walked in here.

"Before I agree, there's something else we should talk about." I hesitate.

"Everything okay?" Jacky's brows knit in confusion.

Passing over the paper, I wait as she silently reads.

Her eyebrows lift.

She looks at me.

I nod.

She tilts her head to the side, pursing her lips.

"This is legitimate?" she asks.

My stomach twists as I nod again.

"How long?"

"Long enough."

She sighs. "Van, he's a player."

"I know."

"I mean, if management finds out…"

They'll protect his job, she's saying. They won't do the same for mine.

"They'll find out sooner or later. We're not hiding it." I nod to the official paperwork. "It's all above-board. We're legitimate now. Dating."

It's not supposed to be a big deal.

So why is my stomach fluttering?

"You're sure you want to do this?" Jacky asks. Concern is sketched on her face.

"I like him," I say simply. "The front office may not like it, but they didn't say it couldn't happen."

Nobody has to ever know that it's not real.

Right?

eight

. . .

Vanessa

A GROAN FILLS THE BAR. I scoff, and Bex rolls her eyes.

"Get with the program, babe," she teases. "It's Saturday. It's time to watch college football."

We're at a Michigan bar in Charlestown, and even though it's nice to be surrounded by the maize and blue, I'm not really feeling it.

"Yeah, well, there's a hockey game on." I turn my attention back to the game on my phone. It's much more interesting, especially because my college football team is out of the playoff picture. After winning the national championship twice in five years (including my senior season), the guys have played particularly poorly the last few years.

"Okay, bitch. Please. We need to talk," Elsy cuts in. "I love hockey. You know I do. But you can't seriously be watching your boy-toy play rather than hanging out here with us and enjoying the evening."

"I am enjoying the evening," I mutter.

"I love Mitch with my whole heart. I do," she says. "But if it came down to watching him play, or living my life? I'd live my damn life, every fucking time. Because I'm worth more than living vicariously through him. He doesn't define my life. I'm worth living for me."

"That's different. Mitch is your best friend. Sven is…"

"He's not the only person in the world," Bex says gently. "I don't care if you're dating or whatever, he doesn't own you. We still get part of you, too."

"I work for the team. It's not just watching my 'boy-toy' as you call him. It's keeping up with my *job*."

It's been two weeks since Sven and I "started dating," as I phrased it to my friends. Not much has changed. I go to work, I do my job, I come home. We don't talk at the training facility. He's busy with his own stuff.

It almost feels anti-climactic. Like… this is it? I just go back to my regular life?

I look down at my phone again, and Sven is on the ice. He's an excellent power forward, and he's on a six-game points streak. He's scored a goal in four out of the last six games since we decided we're dating.

Maybe this isn't such a bad idea after all.

The girls convinced me to go out tonight. Bex's Ph.D. program is year-round, so she doesn't get a lot of time off, and Elsy typically works weekends at the symphony, so it's even more rare that the three of us are able to be together on a Saturday evening. Despite the fact that we all live together, I barely ever see them, and definitely not both at the same time.

My phone vibrates as Boston scores a goal. It's not Sven this time—it's Reynolds, the new guy. I like him. Sometimes he's a little out there, but for the most part, he's chill.

With a sigh, I look through my phone at the text chain I have with Sven. I've reached out a few times, and he only responds with a thumbs-up or a quick one- or two-word phrase. He doesn't have a problem communicating in English; he has a problem communicating in *general*.

I don't know what to make of it.

Is it too much for me to want my fake boyfriend to occasionally talk to me?

Flagging down the waiter, I order another drink.

And another.

Two hours later, I'm more than a little tipsy when I get out of the rideshare. Although I have Sven's address—it was on the relationship declaration form—I haven't been to his place. The neighborhood is not what I expect of a twenty-seven-year old athlete earning several million dollars a season.

We're in a tucked-away corner of Beacon Hill. The brick buildings are picturesque and cute. Sven's building has two flower boxes of purple, blue, and pink asters overflowing from the ground-floor windows. It looks well-maintained, no weeds or dying flowers.

The door behind me slams shut, and I jump.

"Can I help you?"

The voice is older, heavily accented. Its owner is a small woman with dark hair in a braid halfway down her back. She's leaning on a cane, her body clearly frail, but when I meet her eyes, I see she's definitely in control of her faculties.

"I—I'm—" I shiver, pulling my lightweight cardigan around me. The late October wind is colder than I expected.

"You shouldn't be here," she says with finality.

"Oh?" I tilt my head.

"He doesn't want you here."

"Who?"

Her dark eyes narrow. "I think you know who."

The door behind me creaks open, and I look over my shoulder to see Sven standing on the front stoop. A frown mars his beautiful face.

"Vanessa," he says with absolutely no inflection. "Come inside."

The inside of the house is white. There's black wooden flooring and a gray shoe rack in the foyer. There are no pictures, no artwork, nothing on the walls. No clutter. A small console table—black—is off to the side, and even the keys and wallet on it are neatly organized.

"This is your—wow." I take a step further into the townhouse and gape.

His living room is comfortably minimalist. More black wooden flooring. More white walls. A brick fireplace makes up the center focus of the room, and there's a giant flat-screen TV anchored to a wall. A black leather sectional sofa occupies the majority of the room.

There's greenery everywhere. Even after the flowers in the windowsill, I wasn't prepared for the inside of his house to be alive with flora.

"Why are you here?" Sven asks.

He looks tired. He's wearing his post-game suit, though the tie has disappeared, the top two buttons at his throat undone. His blond hair is disheveled, falling loose to his shoulders.

"I—you—we—" I wobble to the left.

"You've been drinking," he says. There's a faint note of disapproval in his voice.

"I'm not working. I'm allowed."

He sighs, turning on his heel and disappearing into the next room. The click of his dress shoes on the floor sends sparks of electricity up my spine. I love a man in a suit. I love a man who knows how to dress.

Following him, I enter the most gorgeous kitchen I have ever seen.

Like the other room, everything is white. White marble countertops, tall white cupboards, and gleaming silver appliances anchor the kitchen. The cabinets are even tall, like they were custom made for him.

Which—frankly, with his salary? They might be.

Sven reaches into a cupboard, withdraws two glasses, and fills them from the water dispenser in the fridge door. He hands one to me and then sinks onto a black wooden stool across the bar from the range.

"Why are you here?" he asks again. This time he sounds cautious.

"We're dating," I tell him.

"Yeah? And?"

"And we need to date." Nodding emphatically, a tuft of hair slips out of my ponytail.

Sven leans forward, tucking the strand behind my ear. "Is that what you want?"

My mouth goes dry.

"I—"

"This is your idea," he says gently. "But I don't want to get you in trouble with work."

"The declaration form is on file. We're fine. It's all above board." I shake my head. "Is that why you haven't talked to me in two weeks?"

He shrugs. "What do you want me to say?"

I stare at him.

He stares back.

Finally, I shake my head. "I'm too drunk for this conversation."

He mutters something under his breath.

"What was that?"

He shakes his head.

"No, really, tell me."

Sven glares at me. The full force of his green eyes bore into me like they can see inside my soul.

"I said, I'm too autistic for this conversation."

nine

. . .

Sven

SHE BLINKS. She does it a few times.

"You're autistic?" she asks.

Holding my breath, I nod.

Vanessa exhales slowly. "That makes so much more sense."

"It does?" I don't want her to think I'm helpless just because sometimes I'm a little awkward in social situations or have difficulty navigating sarcasm and interpersonal relationships.

"Sven," she says, and my stomach lurches at my name on her lips. "We're dating now."

"Okay?"

"That means, we have to talk sometimes."

"I've been in relationships before. I know how this works."

"Yeah, but you've never been in a relationship with me before," Vanessa says. "I need open communication. When I don't hear from my partner for forty-eight hours, not even just a 'hey, I'm alive' message, I get insecure. I start thinking I care about things more than you do."

"But we're only fake dating," I blurt.

Her face falls. "Oh."

"What?"

"I thought…" She trails off.

Leaning toward her, I push the water glass into her hand. She needs to be coherent in order for us to have this conversation.

"Hm?"

"I thought you liked me."

"I do," I say honestly.

"But—" She frowns. "I'm confused."

"So am I," I admit.

"You wanted to ask me out."

I nod. "But you don't date hockey players."

She squints at me. "I am, though. I'm dating you."

"Because you need me. Not because you like me." I can't hide the bitterness in my voice.

To my surprise, Vanessa doesn't seem put off by it. Her face clears, and she reaches for my hand. "Sven—"

Shaking my head, I pull away. "You don't have to pretend, not with me. Let's not make this more than it is."

"But—"

"Do you need to eat anything? Are you hungry?" When I'm drinking, I like greasy food that's definitely not part of my regular diet plan.

Vanessa shakes her head. "I should go."

"It's late." Well after midnight, considering I didn't get home until the clock changed to Sunday morning.

"I know. I'll get a rideshare." She brushes her hair out of her face with uncoordinated limbs.

"You're not getting in a stranger's car at this time of night," I declare.

Her face turns red. "Oh? And who are you to decide that?"

"There's a guest room upstairs. You can sleep it off, and in the morning, I'll drive you home."

Mouth open, she gapes at me like a fish.

Leaning forward, I tip my finger under her chin, closing her mouth.

"Occasionally, I'm a decent person," I tell her quietly. "Just don't tell anyone."

She stares at me for a few beats.

And then she breaks into giggles.

"Oh, Sven," she says, delighted by her good humor, "You are very much a decent person."

"I'm not."

"You are to me. You're helping me out. You—"

Downing the rest of my water, I putter around the kitchen, putting away the glass and clearing the tidy counters.

Vanessa sits on her stool, watching. "Are you upset that I'm here?"

"Why would you think that?"

"Because you're..." She falls silent. "Or are you upset that you have to help me?"

"It's late. You should probably get some rest."

"So that's a yes, then," she decides.

I'm not going to lie to her. But I also don't want her to feel bad about the truth.

Feelings are complicated.

And messy.

And I'm not good at them. I stay in my little corner, isolated from everyone else. Sure, I deal with people when I have to—trainers, teammates, whatever. It's not restful for me to be surrounded by people. I need open space, and Rupert, and my sourdough starter, and—

Vanessa finishes her water, and I take her cup for the dishwasher.

"Are you sure you want me to stay?"

It's not like she'll be sleeping in my bed with me. She'll be all the way across the hall in the guest room.

"It's fine," I tell her stiffly.

She follows me up the stairs. Flicking on the light in the guest room, I double-check that everything is as it should be.

"There's a new toothbrush in the bathroom. You should be able to find everything you need."

Vanessa nods. "Okay. Thanks."

"Good night." Turning on my heel, I make my way across the landing to my bedroom, closing the door behind me.

Scrubbing my hand over my face, I try to recalibrate. It's totally not a big deal that she's here. It's fine. I'm fine. I can just go about my regular routine and—

How the hell am I supposed to lay in bed and jerk off when she's right there?

My shoes go in the closet. Unbuttoning my shirt, I deposit it in the hamper and remove my pants, leaving me in my boxer-briefs. For a moment, I debate covering up more.

She's in the guest room. She won't be in my room. In the morning, I'll get dressed and—

My skin breaks out into goosebumps. I don't like having people in my space. It sets my entire life off-kilter. They're not supposed to be inside my house. This is my safe space, the one place where I can hide from everyone in the world. Not even Hildy has been to my house; I always go to hers.

The only person who has ever come over is Brigitte, the med student who watches over Rupert while I'm gone, and we are never here at the same time; she has a copy of my schedule, so she knows when she's needed, and all communication is handled via email.

The only reason I even have a guest room is because I needed someone to watch out for Rupert. If it wasn't for that, I'd be fine with a studio. Okay, maybe a one-bedroom apartment. I like having the door closed while I'm asleep.

My heart is hammering. Despite my earlier shower at the arena, my skin is slicked with sweat.

Pulling my tablet out of my nightstand drawer, I turn on one of my favorite videos. Even though I'm always alone, I never watch it with sound. Hearing the actors' faked moans and groans turns me off.

As I slick my hand with lube and draw my cock out of my briefs, I wonder about the propriety of doing this while she's right there. It's not like I'm inviting her to come in and help me out. I don't even want her to help me out.

I don't think I do.

I don't know.

Maybe?

No. No, I—

Yeah.

I do.

I really want her to.

But that's not what we are. We're fake dating. We're not a real couple where we can discuss physical needs in a rational and clinical way.

My attention strays from the video, the blue-tinted light bright in the dark room. As usual, my mind drifts to one of my favorite memories.

Weddings aren't exactly my idea of fun, and Jackson's wedding was no exception. I was seated at the single and underage table.

And then she was there.

We drank.

We danced.

She flirted.

We went back to her room.

And then—

My cock grows stiffer at the memory, and as I stroke myself, I think back to the way it felt to have her in my arms, the easy way she talked to me all night long, the way she seemed like she was actually — genuinely — interested in me.

Our first kiss was on the dance floor. She took the lead there. She initiated.

She wanted it, too.

She wanted it as much as I did.

Cupping my balls, I roll them in my hand and then slide two fingers under to my taint, the way she did that night. I'd never known I was so sensitive there until her.

She taught me more than I could ever expect.

And as I touch myself to the memory of that night nine years ago, my thoughts drift to the woman on the other side of my wall.

Vanessa Morgan.

She's been off limits for so long. First, I was with someone. Then, once that ended, she made clear she didn't get involved with hockey players.

But she is involved now. She is dating me.

She said so herself. She certainly seemed confused when I blurted out that we're just dating for appearances.

Shifting my grip, my strokes slow as I consider the possibilities here. She's so close but still so far away. How do I transverse this distance between us? How do I prove to her my intentions are pure? How do I convince her that I want to protect her from Andrews?

My cock jerks, and I curse under my breath, remembering the way she sucked me down. Maybe my intentions aren't so pure after all…

Pleasure bursts along my spine, coiling low in my gut, and as my cock spills into my hand, I let out the quietest grunt, and then my body sags with a sigh.

My bones feel loosey-goosey, like marshmallows. Or maybe like Twizzlers. Ooh, Twizzlers sound good right now.

It takes considerable effort to get to my feet, and as I clean up, the bone-deep exhaustion hits. I'm so fucking tired.

It's not that I'm sleepy, although I am. It's more of a soul-crushing, spirit-destroying, body-melting kind of exhaustion.

My body is bruised from the game, my muscles ache, and

I have a scratch on the inside of my forearm from a high-sticking penalty that didn't get called.

I don't know how to do this.

How do I tell the woman I'm faking a relationship with that I want it to be real?

How do I tell the woman I've had feelings for since our one night together almost a decade ago that she is still incredibly meaningful to me?

How do I tell the woman I called my engagement off over that once she walked back into my life, I couldn't stand the thought of being with anyone else?

ten

. . .

Vanessa

THE HANGOVER WAKES me up before I'm ready. My brain pounds inside my skull, desperate for freedom. Can brains ever be truly free of our skulls?

Fuck, am I still drunk?

Lurching toward the en suite bathroom, I take care of personal business and then crawl back into the nice and comfortable bed.

Why did I come to Sven?

And more importantly, why did he want me to stay?

I wish I knew how to read him. He's as opaque as a brick wall. Hell, sometimes I think he might be a brick wall.

The bed I'm in is plush with thick blankets; white linens, white duvet, and white blankets. The walls are painted a light gray, just a shade darker than white, and there's a spotless white rug on the black wooden floors. A small aloe plant sits on the bedside table, and there's an orange and pink orchid on top of the dresser. Not a lot of greenery otherwise, unlike downstairs.

The floorboards creak and the pipes run. Sven must be up. I can hear him puttering around in his room, and when he opens his door, his footsteps pause outside mine before descending the stairs.

I wait a few minutes. Briefly, I debate climbing out the window. That's a little much, I rationalize. He knows I'm here. He expects me to be here.

I can't run from this any longer.

Making my way downstairs, I'm surprised again at the amount of greenery in the stark black and white apartment. The blinds are drawn and the midmorning sunlight sends sunbeams across the room.

Something hurtles toward me, and I shriek and duck, covering my head with my hands. I used to play lacrosse, but that was with heavy padding, a mouth and face guard, and a stick to protect me. I'm not used to things flying at me anymore.

"Rupert," Sven says sharply.

Shit. He sounds pissed.

Did he throw—

There's a flapping noise above me. And as I uncover my head, I find the wide wingspan of a gray bird hovering above me. It's about the size of a football, maybe a little longer, with a shocking crimson tail. Beady golden eyes are focused on me.

"Good girl," the bird caws. "Good baby girl."

It *talks?!*

"Rupert, come," Sven demands.

And to my surprise, the bird flies over to him, perching on his shoulder.

"I'm sorry," Sven says to me. His accent is stronger in the mornings. "She's not used to strangers."

"She?"

"This is Rupert." Reaching upward, he runs a finger along the bird's dark beak, and it nuzzles the appendage. "She gets pretty free range inside. If she makes you uncomfortable, I can put her in the pen."

"No, it's fine," I manage. "I just wasn't expecting the attack."

"Good girl," the parrot squawks. "Rupert, good girl."

"Yes, you're my good girl," he murmurs to the bird, who rubs her beak against his cheek.

Damn it. I want him to call *me* his good girl.

How the fuck am I getting jealous of a goddamn bird?

"Rupert is a girl?"

He nods. "The previous owner didn't know until she laid an egg. They were quite surprised."

"Are there any more birds flying around here I should be aware of?"

He shakes his head, and Rupert squawks again and nibbles on his ear.

It's only then that I realize he is in the middle of cooking. There's a carton of eggs, some vegetables chopped in small ramekins, and what smells like fresh bread baking.

"Good morning," he says conversationally. "How do you like your eggs?"

I blink.

"You're making eggs?"

Confused, he nods.

"With a bird on your shoulder?"

Sven quirks a smile. "Well, they weren't hers. They're from the store."

"That doesn't bother you?"

"She eats them, too." He shrugs, and Ruperts lets out a grumbly squawk at her perch moving beneath her feet. I see the way her talons grip into his shoulder and he winces.

"Good baby girl," he murmurs to the bird, who butts her head against his and then takes off. She clips his head with her wing as she flies toward the kitchen sink. A black wooden perch is set in front of the closed window, and she settles there, making herself comfortable.

Sven gestures to the espresso machine in the corner, beside

which is a simple coffee pot. "Coffee will be ready soon, or I have a selection of tea if you'd prefer."

"Coffee is great, thanks." He has everything out and prepared. "Is there anything I can help with?"

"How do you like your eggs?" he repeats.

"Um…"

"Scrambled? Over easy? Hard boiled? That may take a minute." He quirks his smile at me, and my stomach flutters.

I'm just hungry. It's the hangover.

Except my head doesn't really hurt. I'm a little queasy, sure. Altogether, I don't feel all that bad.

"Whatever you're doing is fine." I perch on a barstool. The oven is on, a timer counting down. "Are you baking something?"

His eyebrows go up. "Yes?"

Most of the professional hockey players I know have someone else around to do the cooking. And baking? Fuck, I'm surprised any of them even know how to turn on the oven.

Sven starts cracking eggs into a clear glass bowl. He gets through three-quarters of the dozen before he starts scrambling. From little pinch bowls, he rains salt and pepper into the bowl, then adds milk and starts scrambling with a whisk.

Like, an actual fucking whisk.

I'm a grown-ass adult, and I've been living on my own since I graduated college, and I still don't have a fucking whisk in my kitchen.

And this asshole? He's a professional hockey player, and he busts it out? He's cooking? And baking?

What is this, the freaking Twilight Zone?

The coffee pot chimes, and Sven pauses the whisking to pull down two white porcelain cups from a meticulously organized cabinet.

"So you like to cook?" I ask.

"I have to eat, don't I?" He looks over his shoulder at me with that half-smile.

"A lot of guys hire it out."

He shrugs. "I'm not them."

"No," I say slowly. "I suppose you're not."

He pours a cup of coffee, then walks around the center island and deposits it in front of me.

"I've got almond milk and sugar, and there's flavored creamer in the fridge."

I blink. "You have flavored coffee creamer?"

That is so not allowed on the elite hockey player diet plan.

"It's Brigitte's."

"Who's that?" Another bird? Another girlfriend?

No, he said he wasn't seeing anyone when we hatched this cockamamie plan.

"Rupert's house sitter," he says. "She does some work around the place, too."

"Oh?"

"Cleaning, laundry, grocery shopping." He makes a face. "I hate grocery shopping."

Okay, irrational jealousy, calm the fuck down.

"Yeah, I suppose you would." He probably gets mobbed by fans, even in his quiet little neighborhood. "So Brigitte—is she here often?"

"Whenever I'm gone overnight." He cocks his head. "Everything is handled by email. I put what I need in a note and she handles it."

Now it makes sense why there were fancy soaps and shampoos in the bathroom and clothes in the dresser. If she's his regular house sitter, it would make sense that she keeps some things here.

Making my way to the fridge, I'm surprised by how clean everything is inside. It's full of fresh vegetables, already chopped and prepared in glass containers. A shelf contains brown paper packages labeled chicken and salmon, and a small basket of fancy European cheeses.

He has a porn-worthy refrigerator.

On the door is a bottle of Oreo-flavored creamer. Damn. I might like Brigitte. First she uses nice-smelling soaps, now she drinks good-tasting coffee?

Pouring some in my cup, I watch as the dark liquid joy turns a pale off-brown color. Now that I'm not playing lacrosse and watching every fucking calorie I eat, coffee with creamer is one of my favorite indulgences.

Sven moves to the eight-burner range. It's top of the line, as are the rest of his appliances. Then again, if he likes to cook, that's not much of a surprise.

"I feel like I should help. What can I do to help?"

Just as the words leave my mouth, the oven dings.

"Could you get that?" Sven pauses as he adds some butter to the pan.

Using the black pot holders beside the oven, I open the door and am assaulted by the heavenly scent of freshly baked bread.

My mouth waters. If this is what sleeping at Sven's house is like, sign me the fuck up.

The dutch oven is heavier than I expected. Sven moves behind me, closing the oven door.

"You can set it here." He points to the closest burner, which is the farthest from where he's cooking.

"You bake bread?"

Sven shrugs. "It's tasty."

I blink at him. It's tasty?

"There's no point in keeping a starter if I don't exercise it regularly."

"Who are you?" I blurt.

His easy smile goes blank in an instant.

Quickly, I backtrack: "Fuck. No. I just—"

Scrubbing a hand over my face, I try to hide my wince.

"You're not what I expected," I admit.

"What did you expect?" His tone is careful as he adds broccoli and peppers to the sizzling pan.

"Just… not this."

He looks over his shoulder at me, clearly unimpressed.

I shrug. "Fine. I expected some asshole dude-bro hockey player with a stick up his ass."

Sven snorts, mumbling something in Swedish.

"You're not what I expected," I repeat. "And I'm so glad for that."

eleven

. . .

Vanessa

WE SIT at the counter and eat our breakfast. The bread has to cool, so it's not ready to be sliced, he explains. He also doesn't have a kitchen table by design—he doesn't like them. I don't quite get it, but that's okay, because it's not something I have to understand. It's his life, his house, his kitchen. He can do whatever the fuck he wants with it.

"What are you up to today?" I ask as I finish off my eggs. I was hungrier than I thought, because they practically disappeared as soon as I sat down.

Today is a day off—the league-mandated day off—because they've had so many consecutive days of games and training.

Sven shrugs. "Bake some more bread, maybe go for a swim."

The training facility doesn't have a pool. I wonder where he goes. The guys generally don't go to non-team facilities because of the risk of getting mobbed by fans. Even the most stoic of bodybuilders turn into giggling fans in the presence of the hockey team.

I wait for him to ask what I'm doing, but he doesn't.

Does he not care? Or does he not realize that's the expected way to continue the conversation?

Sven is absorbed by his meal. He takes his coffee with a splash of almond milk. Rupert is perched on his shoulder. Every so often, he offers her a piece of the eggs from his palm, and she guzzles it down.

He's surprisingly affectionate when it comes to the bird.

I should probably stop calling her "the bird."

"What kind of bird is Rupert?" I ask. The name intrigues me. You don't find a lot of Ruperts nowadays, especially not in female birds.

Sven trails a finger over her neck. "She's an African Gray Parrot. She's not allowed to leave the house and all the windows are screened so she can't get loose. Other than that, she gets pretty much free rein of the place."

"She wasn't out last night?" It's more of a question than a statement.

"Rupert goes to bed pretty early. Her cage is in the living room. She has a perch upstairs, but I don't sleep so well when she's in my room." His cheeks tint pink.

Even though he didn't ask, mentally, I run through my schedule for the rest of the week. I didn't have to work yesterday —Scott was on shift—and after Tuesday's home game, I'm supposed to travel with the team to Pittsburgh for my first road trip. Wednesday and Thursday, I'll work from the team's hotel, handling anything the staff requires. After Thursday night's game, we head on to Philadelphia for a quick back-to-back game.

We're scheduled to get back to Boston Friday night—or rather, Saturday morning, since the private plane doesn't leave until close to midnight. It's a quick hour-and-a-half flight. Doesn't make getting home from work at two o'clock in the morning any more appealing.

At least being on the same schedule as the players will give me some consistency. Right now, my schedule can be pretty volatile as Jacky, Scott, and I rotate to provide coverage. Since I'm filling in for Jacky (and she's handling my duties back at the arena), it makes sense for me to absorb most of the travel.

And—well, it gets me closer to Sven.

The man sitting in front of me clears his throat. "There's a party."

"Oh?" I've never known him to be interested in parties.

"The team." Sven focuses on a point somewhere behind me and to the left. "Next week, there's a Halloween party."

"Oh."

Is he asking me to go with him?

"What sort of costume do you like?"

I think he is.

But—I tilt my head.

"What's wrong?" Sven asks.

"What do you have in mind?" I deflect.

"Everyone does couple's costumes," he says with a frown.

So he is asking me.

Or—well, he's presuming I'll go with him.

He's right, of course. I'll go with him. I want to go with him, even beyond the expectation that we are there together.

"Do you want funny, scary, or sexy?" I ask.

Sven wrinkles his nose. "Not scary."

"We could do a celebrity couple, or someone from a movie, or—"

"I don't care," he says. "Whatever you want."

"No. You don't get to do that," I tell him, crossing my arms over my chest. "This may be a fake relationship, but I won't do all of the emotional labor. We both have to carry the weight."

He blinks at me. "Okay. All I'm saying is, I don't have a preference, so whatever interests you, I'm already agreeing to it. You don't have to run it by me, you can pick whatever you want."

"That's still me doing the emotional labor."

"It is?" He looks genuinely confused.

"Your not caring means that I have to care, because otherwise nobody does and it won't get done."

Sven pauses.

"What?" I snap the word more harshly than I intended.

"I never thought of it that way," he says quietly. "I thought I was helping."

Some of my coolness thaws. He's really not trying to be difficult.

"You have to tell me," he says. When I open my mouth, he lifts his hand. "It's emotional labor for you to educate me. I realize. But I need you to tell me—one time—and then I won't repeat the behavior again. I don't always recognize the patterns until they're brought to my attention."

I consider this.

He's trying. He cares.

"I haven't been in a relationship for a long time," Sven says slowly. "I don't know where the boundaries are here. I like rules. I like structure. And this thing with us…"

I wait.

"I don't know what the rules are," he finishes. "I need to know."

"Well, we're dating."

"Yes, but what does that mean?" His eyes are intent on my face. "Do you come to the games? Do you sit in the box, or on the ice, or are you in the pit with everyone? The guys who go out after the game—are we supposed to go with them?"

"Wow. You're, like, really wigging out."

"I need rules," Sven says simply. "In the absence of rules, I default to the norm."

"I didn't go to last night's game, but I saw your goal in the second period," I tell him. "We were out at a bar and I was watching the game on my phone."

His forehead wrinkles. "We?"

"Me and my two roommates," I explain. "Bex and I played lacrosse in college together, and she met Elsy in grad school. Bex's brother is in the league and Elsy's best friend plays, too."

He quirks an eyebrow. "Oh?"

"Wyatt Whitney and Nick Mitchell."

Sven lets out a low whistle. "I know Whitney. He's formidable."

"He's a teddy bear for his little sister." I shrug. "He used to buy us alcohol in college. Every time he came to visit, the fridge was magically full of beer and wine."

"And Mitchell?"

"I've only met him once, when his team played Boston last year. He took Elsy and me out for drinks. He's... fine, I guess." I shrug. I hardly know the guy. "It's kind of funny that the three of us all have hockey connections. We didn't realize it at the time. I was already working for the team when Bex and Elsy moved to the city."

He hums. I can't tell what that means.

"Do you go back to Sweden every summer?"

"Only for visa requirements." Sven frowns. "I don't talk to my family much. They don't like me."

"Oh, I'm sure they—"

"My sister is a lawyer, and my brothers are doctors and in business," he says. "I'm the disappointment."

I gape at him. "You're an elite hockey player."

He shrugs. "So?"

"So you're... like, you're an amazing hockey player."

"Athletics are nothing to be proud of," he says. His voice lacks any tone or inflection.

"What the fuck? Who the hell told you that?" My voice is rising in pitch, and I have the strong urge to punch someone.

"Good baby girl," Rupert says, staring at me.

"My father," Sven says.

"Well, he can fuck right off," I declare.

To my surprise, Sven quirks a small smile. "Yes. That is why I don't go back to Sweden much."

"Don't you miss it?"

"Not terribly, no." His voice is dry. "In the off season, I might go on holiday for a bit, but then it's time to recover and prepare for the next season."

"You don't get a break?"

Even the Logistics team gets a few weeks off after the close of the season.

He shrugs. "I've never found anything I would rather do more than hockey."

I stare at him, trying to ascertain if he's being truthful, and I realize he doesn't know how to be any other way.

"So, rules?" I ask, circling back to our earlier conversation that neither of us finished.

"Rules."

I nod. "Okay. Let's talk about it."

twelve

. . .

Sven

THERE IS OFTEN a strange routine to the inconsistency in my schedule. Regardless of where I play, most home games start at seven o'clock, which means they end close to ten, and we're on the plane around midnight. Time zones may be different, but the hour remains the same. I find a lot of solace in that.

But then, there are times the games start an hour earlier or later, it messes everything up. On weekends, sometimes we play a matinee, when we start just after noon but have to get to the arena ass-crack early. Some days we play back to back, and some weeks we only play one or two games instead of four or five.

These are the times when there's too much variation.

In general, I'm not a night owl. Mornings are my preference. But I don't get to have a choice, not really, not when hockey dictates my schedule.

Vanessa is coming on the road trip with us. I know this, because she texted me the other day and said "I'm going on the next road trip," and I typed back "okay," and I also said "your hair looks very nice today and I want to kiss you."

Except I deleted that last part.

I don't think I'm supposed to tell my fake girlfriend that I think she's pretty and I want to kiss her. Even though I think she's pretty and want to kiss her, like, all the fucking time.

We had the rules conversation the morning after she stayed at my place. And up until now, there have been very strict boundaries. She stays home, and I go away, and then I come back, and she's there looking irresistible, and I go back to my house and masturbate to the memory of our one-night stand all those years ago.

After our Tuesday night game, it's time to head to Pittsburgh. I only know we're going to Pittsburgh because tomorrow we have a team dinner at the same bougie steakhouse we always go to, and also because it says so on the team email.

Following my teammates, I board the plane and sit in row 13. Nobody else likes row 13. I do. The number makes me happy. Everyone else's avoidance of it only adds to its appeal. They give me a wide berth.

Vanessa boards the plane with a group of other staffers. There's Patrice and Angelica, and Joaquin-with-a-J, and George-with-a-G.

Her eyes meet mine from the entrance to the plane, and immediately I feel like a weight has been lifted off my shoulders. I haven't seen her in a few hours. I missed her.

Fuck. I need to chill out. I need to cool down. I need—

She's approaching. Quick. Pretend like—

Apprehension covers her face like a mask.

Silently, I tip my head to the seat beside me.

She hesitates.

I catch sight of Andrews and the rest of the equipment staff boarding the plane. My good mood sours.

Ducking into the row, Vanessa takes the open seat, leaving the middle seat empty. Jenkins, sitting in the row ahead of me, swivels his head to stare at her.

I glare at him, and he flinches.

"This okay?" she whispers. Her hands are shaking.

Taking her hand in mine, I squeeze her fingers, rubbing my thumb over the back of her knuckles.

Jenkins' eyes go as big as saucers.

Andrews glares at me.

Good. My work here is done.

"How was your evening?" I ask quietly.

"Good. You played well."

"Thanks." I manage half a smile. Even though I didn't get a goal, I did manage two assists, so I feel comfortably pleased with my performance. "You watched?"

"I always watch. I just don't always get to see it from the stands." She shifts in her seat. "I was finishing up some paperwork in the back office. Getting ready. Usually I don't travel with the team."

Inclining my head, I wonder what's changed. Scott, the other Logistics Coordinator, was with us on our last trip. It didn't strike me as abnormal until she appeared today.

"Hey, Van," Jenkins says, nodding at her.

Her eyes flick to him. "Hi."

"You're here with us?"

She gives him a tight-lipped smile. "Looks like, yeah."

Andrews stows his stuff in the compartment above row 13 on the left side of the plane, sitting on the aisle. It's like he can't possibly bear to be apart from her. Clingy asshole.

On the other hand, I can't really blame him. I don't want to be separated from her, either.

Despite our relationship declaration form officially being on file, I don't think anyone really knows yet. About us, that is. We won't get in trouble with management or ownership, but none of the guys know. None of the staff.

I guess they're about to find out.

"Nessie," Andrews says, nodding at her.

She rolls her eyes. "Hi, Robby." She turns to face me, her

hand squeezing mine so tightly it almost cuts off my circulation. "How's Rupert?"

"Already asleep for the night." She goes to sleep around sundown each night, even on the days I'm home in the evening. "Brigitte is with her."

Vanessa smiles softly.

"What are you up to tomorrow?" I ask. We have practice from ten to two and then free time before the team dinner at that stupid steakhouse. Thursday, we'll be at the training facility most of the morning, then time for a pregame nap before we head back to start preparing for the evening's matchup.

"Just some paperwork. I have a half-day," she says. "Now that I'm on the road more, Jacky is reallocating some of my daily responsibilities to compensate."

I don't really know what she does. I mean, I know she works in logistics. I don't know what that means, though. When I signed here, all of the details were handled by some dude named Tim and my then-fiancée. They found me an apartment in the North End—which I hated—and moved all my stuff from Arizona and unpacked it. All I had to do was show up.

When we broke up, Marika was the one to move out since the season had already started. After an abysmally short playoff run, my realtor closed on my current house and coordinated the movers.

I don't know what's going to happen when I leave Boston. If I leave Boston. I've got a year left on my contract, and even though I hope to get one more long-term contract, it's highly likely that I'll be unable to.

I like this team. I like this city. I've got Hildy and Brigitte and… Vanessa.

Detangling my hand from hers, I put up the two armrests dividing us. She scoots a little closer—not much, just a little.

Because the flight is so short, there's no point in changing out of my suit into casual clothes, only to put the suit back on an hour later. For longer flights, we're allowed to wear comfortable clothes. Pre- and post-game, though, we're to wear our suits. I've removed my jacket and rolled up my sleeves, the only concession to comfort.

Vanessa yawns, covering her mouth with her hand.

"Tired?" I ask, fighting the urge to take her hand back.

I wince. Of course she's tired. She just yawned.

She nods. "Bex and I went to a new workout class at an obscene hour this morning. I didn't think that through."

"At least tomorrow you can sleep in."

"I've still got a lot of work to do," she says.

"Well, if you want to rest now, I have a shoulder to lean on," I offer.

Why? *Why* did I say that?

But when Vanessa smiles up at me, my heart starts to flutter, and maybe…

"Thanks. That'd be nice," she says quietly.

After the flight takes off, she moves to the middle seat, drawing her legs up to the empty seat beside her.

Immediately, I thread my arm across her shoulders, my hand on her waist, and she yawns again, squirming closer to me. Her hair smells like coconut, and her light floral perfume does dangerous things to my senses.

And when she sets her hand on my knee?

Everything goes haywire. My blood rushes south very, very quickly, and I swallow thickly, trying to avoid disturbing her.

"I'm just going to sleep for a little bit," she says. Her eyes can barely stay open. "A power nap. Ten minutes."

"I'll wake you when it's time," I promise. "Get some rest."

thirteen

. . .

Sven

THE GUYS STARE at me when I enter the team room for breakfast. I ignored them last night, especially after Vanessa exited the plane ahead of me.

Taking my now customary seat at MacGregor's table, he looks up at me with curiosity scrawled on his face.

"What?" I grunt.

He smiles and shakes his head. "You're full of surprises, aren't you?"

I shrug, pulling out my phone for my daily news site perusal.

Even with my back to the door, I'm acutely aware of the exact moment she walks into the room. Her floral perfume precedes her in the best possible way. My heart starts to pound, my blood rushes, and I have to cough to clear my throat because swallowing is impossible.

She fills a plate and approaches my table.

"Good morning," she says brightly.

"Good morning, Vanessa," MacGregor says, hiding a smile. "You're traveling now?"

She nods. "Jacky can't travel for a bit, so I'm filling in on the road. You mind if I sit here?"

Her eyes aren't on MacGregor, though. They're on me.

Nodding, my eyes flick down to the empty three seats between me and the assistant captain.

She sits directly next to me.

"Good morning," I say quietly, flipping my phone down on the table.

Vanessa leans toward me, then pauses. I squeeze her shoulder, unsure how to convey how glad I am that she's here.

"Was that Rupert?" She nods to my phone.

"Yes. When we're away, I check on her every morning."

Taking my phone, I unlock the screen and show her the video feed. My bird is free to fly about the living room. She's gliding through the air, seemingly playing the limbo with a vine that stretches across the room.

"Oh, she's so cute." Vanessa leans closer, looking at the screen. "Does she know you check in on her?"

"I think so." When I sit alone and have my headphones in, I can turn on the sound and talk back to her, but I know it scares Brigitte when I do, so I try to time it for when she is out of the house. She's cleaning the house today; that's what she always does on the first day I'm gone.

Vanessa takes a sip of her coffee, sighing happily.

"How'd you sleep?" I ask.

"Good. You?"

I would have slept better with her beside me.

I don't say that, though.

"Not bad. I'm used to the late night, though."

She hums softly. "I'll get used to it. It's just a new routine."

After breakfast, we have a team meeting. Vanessa disappears with the other support staff—she doesn't need to hear about Pittsburgh's intricate defensive plays—but comes down to the lobby as we're about to head to the arena.

We get some stares when she sits beside me on the bus. Nobody says anything, though.

Do I want them to? I don't want to hide it. I just don't think we need to announce it.

The locker room is loud, and it gets conspicuously quiet when I walk into the room.

"What the fuck is going on, Larsson?" Pope demands. He's a defenseman with the personality of a prickly bear, 6'7", and as big as a brick shit-house.

"What are you talking about?" I keep my tone neutral as I reach for my gear.

"Morgan travels with us for the first time all season, and when she does, she sits next to you?" he demands.

I shrug. "She likes me."

Lewis scoffs. "Is that all it is?"

Even though we have clearance from the team, even though it's all above board, it feels strange to confirm our fake relationship without her here.

"She doesn't hook up with players," Sinclair says. "Like, distinctly off-limits, get booted from the team if you touch her."

"I'll take that under advisement," I say neutrally.

Clark shakes his head. "You're risking career suicide, dude."

What I don't tell him is that she would be worth the risk. Eleven out of ten times, she's worth it.

———

As I go about my regular routine, my mind drifts to Vanessa. She's working. I wonder what she's doing. I don't exactly understand her job, just that she likes it and without her, the team wouldn't run nearly as smoothly.

She's not on the bus back to the hotel after practice, but at dinner, she's sitting at a table with the other staff members. I sit at the end of the table and keep to myself. I'd much rather sit beside her than next to Clark and Jenkins.

Some of the guys head to a bar after dinner. I don't join them. I don't know if she does. I'm not in the mood to drink or try to get laid—as if. I'm ready to relax and let myself rest.

My phone chimes with a message. Vanessa's name is on the screen.

"I'm bored," she texted. "What are you up to?"

"Watching a movie," I reply.

"Can I join you?"

I send her my room number.

Springing out of bed, I wash my face and brush my teeth. A glob of toothpaste lands on my chest and I whip off my shirt, ready to find a new one.

Right then, there's a knock on my door. I open to find Vanessa wearing casual sweats and a sweatshirt, her hair tied up in a bun.

"Is this okay?" she asks.

Without hesitating, I take her hand and pull her inside the room.

"What are you doing here?" I ask.

She shrugs. "I just… I didn't want to be alone."

"I'm glad I could help, then."

"You didn't want to go to the bar?"

"Not my scene. I only go when I have to."

Vanessa's eyes trail over my bare chest and down to my loose joggers. "Am I overdressed?"

I shake my head. "I can find a shirt if you'd prefer."

She sets her hand on my pec, curling it over my chest to my shoulder. "Why are you still single?"

"I'm not," I tell her. "We're dating. Remember?"

She smirks. "Yeah, well, until then. Why haven't they snatched you up yet?"

"Most of the time I'm on my own. I like being alone. Generally, I prefer it."

"Oh. I can leave." She removes her hand from my skin, and I reach for her, pulling her hand back to my shoulder.

"I'd rather be with you than be by myself," I correct.

Her soft smile makes me smile, too. Except I'm grinning like a loon. I can't stop. My face won't go back to normal.

There are two double beds in the room, so I'm surprised when she gets into my bed, the one with the tablet and the covers rolled down.

"Okay, I'm going to be completely transparent here," Vanessa says, pulling the sheets up to her waist.

I wait.

"I really liked cuddling with you on the plane last night, and I want to do it again," she announces.

My mouth gets dry. "Okay…"

"Also, it would help if you didn't flinch every time I touch you." She doesn't sound upset; she's hiding a smile, her eyes bright.

It would help if I didn't get hard every time she touches me.

Slowly, I crawl into the bed beside her, and immediately Vanessa moves toward me. She arranges my arms until she's enveloped in the circle of them, her back to my front, her head on my bicep.

"That's better," she announces.

"What did you want to watch?" I pick up the tablet.

"Whatever you're watching." She squirms closer. "I just want to be held by you."

Selecting the first movie I can find— a superhero movie from two summers ago—I lie down on the bed and curl my arm around her belly, holding her close.

She's soft and she smells good, and having her in my arms feels right. Like I was made for the sole purpose of holding her.

———

Again, I don't see her all day. She's not at breakfast, and she's not on the bus to the training facility. I don't know where she is. Did she get in trouble for visiting me last night? Nothing even happened!

It's when we're warming up and getting ready for the game that I finally see her again. She's wearing a team sweatshirt and leggings with her favorite combat boots. Her blonde hair is pulled into a loose braid over one shoulder. She enters the team's workout room with a pinched smile on her face.

"Hey," she says, making eye contact.

"Hi."

"Can we talk?"

I'm conspicuously aware of the guys' attention on us as I get up from foam rolling and follow her out of the room.

"What's going on?" I ask as she finds a quiet alcove.

"I just wanted to check in," Vanessa says, biting her lip.

"Okay…"

"I haven't seen you at all today."

"It's game day."

"I know. It's—" She blows out a breath. "I don't want to make things uncomfortable for you with the rest of the team."

"You're not."

"Jenkins on the plane… MacGregor at breakfast…"

"They can go fuck themselves," I declare.

Her eyes go big.

"Everything is legal and approved. They don't matter," I tell her. "Are you getting flack for it?"

"Pope saw me leave your room last night," she admits.

My stomach sinks. "Oh."

"He was… well, he's a dick on a good day," she continues.

"Yeah. Tell me about it." I shake my head. "Are you okay?"

"I'm fine. I just wanted to check on you. Make sure he wasn't giving you shit."

Not for this, not today.

"I'm used to ignoring him," I deflect.

I want to pull her into my arms and hold her. I want to kiss her and never let her go.

But whatever happened last night added to the fact that we're supposed to be fake dating—only for appearance's sake —it leaves me wondering if what I feel for her is reciprocated. I think it is, especially after her behavior on the plane and last night in my room.

But I've been wrong before.

I can't risk falling for her even more and losing her. I have to keep my distance emotionally. It's been easy until now because there was a clear boundary in place.

The locker room door opens, and I hear footsteps.

"Okay. Well—I have to go," Vanessa says. She pauses, then rises to her toes and presses a soft kiss to my cheek. "Have a good game, Sven."

Maybe I'm not wrong now.

fourteen

. . .

Vanessa

HE SCORED a goal and an assist last night. After a quick post-game dinner in the locker room, the guys board the plane to Philly. As much as I want to, I can't sit beside Sven— Patrice, the social media coordinator, wants to chat about some promos we're doing tomorrow.

I eat breakfast hours before the players are up, and I'm already at the arena and getting my regular job duties done by the time the players show up for prep.

During pre-game skate, I'm standing at the bench with Joaquin, who is filming some footage of the behind-the-scenes.

An orange jersey skates past us. We're on our side of the ice, so I don't give it much thought until it appears again, spraying us with ice.

"Hey, Van," he says, taking off his helmet.

My eyes go wide, and I grin. "Wyatt!"

He grabs for me, and I let the buffoon hug me. I almost forgot he played for this city.

There's a murmur from the staff behind the bench. They probably think I'm fraternizing with the enemy or some bull- shit like that. It couldn't be further from the truth.

"Haven't seen you in a while, chicky," he says. He smells like sweat, even though the game hasn't started yet.

"Yeah. You're taking care of yourself?"

My roommate's brother grins. "Well, you know me."

"Yeah. I do. That's why I have to check."

Wyatt smirks. "You don't usually travel with the team."

"Things change," I say shortly. Out of the corner of my eye, I see Sven skating around the ice, glaring in our direction. He fires a puck toward the net and Lewis dives out of the way.

"So it's not just to see me?" Wyatt winks.

"Yes, definitely, it's all a ploy to see you," I tell him dryly. Pope, stretching his hamstring nearby, looks over at us curiously. "You're ridiculous. Glad to see you haven't changed, dude."

"You should have called me. We could have hung out while you're here."

"We're on a back-to-back. Got in last night and I've been here all day."

Wyatt shakes his head. "Next time. I won't be up in Boston until January, I think."

"We'll sit down and compare schedules later," I promise. "You should get back to your side of the ice. Your coach will get pissed."

"Yeah, maybe." He runs his hands through his hair. "Take good care of Bex, you hear?"

"She can take care of herself." She's close to thirty and working on a doctorate degree. She's a functional adult.

"She's my baby sister," he says. "I worry about her."

"You don't have to."

"I do, though." Wyatt sighs. "I've got to go."

He ducks down and kisses me on the cheek, then pats me on the head like a child.

The guys continue to warm up, and I watch as Sven

shoots an absolute laser at the goal. Lewis doesn't attempt to block it—he lets the missile fly by him.

"Let's try not to decapitate our goalie, thanks," Coach Turner calls.

"What's up his ass?" Joaquin mutters.

"No clue," I say, but something skates across my brain, scratching a spot that whispers he didn't like Wyatt's attention on me.

I shrug it off because I've barely seen him all day. It's been a busy time—I've barely had enough time to breathe. From the time we touched down in Philly last night, and I crashed into bed the second my hotel room door closed, to waking up this morning, it's been go-go-go.

I don't know that I'm cut out for a life on the road.

Or, maybe, I just need to take a pre-game nap like the athletes.

With the athletes?

Well, with one athlete in particular.

Sven is big and imposing in his gear. The skates make him even taller, and the pads broaden his big chest, and when his eyes lock on mine from across the ice... my heart goes pitter-pat, and my pussy clenches around emptiness.

It's been a long time since I've gotten laid. Even though I'm capable of taking care of any physical needs on my own, I do miss the physical intimacy of having a partner. Being held. Sleeping beside someone. Spending a leisurely morning naked in bed.

Lying in his bed, curled up in the circle of his arms... it was like all my thoughts and fears went away. I wasn't tired from the early wake-up call, and my feet didn't hurt from running around all day, and I wasn't worried about ten thousand possibilities of "what if."

I could just breathe.

Barely paying attention to the movie he put on last night, I was more preoccupied by the warmth of his bare chest against my back, and his strong hand rubbing my arm, and the spicy fresh scent of his soap.

I like him.

I knew he was attractive. I knew he was a nice guy.

But I wasn't supposed to develop feelings for my fake boyfriend.

The first night of this trip, the only thing I wanted to do was be with him. A few of the guys had invited me to the bar. Patrice and Angelica went out with some friends in town.

And me? All I'd wanted was to see Sven, talk to him, cuddle with him, and just… exist in his space. I wanted him.

Fuck. I think I want this to be more than it is.

Blowing out a breath, I rub at my forehead. This is confusing. Feelings are confusing. Why do I have to feel this? I just want—

Him.

I want him.

With perfect clarity, I know it as well as I know my name.

How did it take me so long to see it?

Sven rushes to a stop in front of the boards, dropping his gloves to the ice. I step forward and he cages me in, his hands on either side of mine. His eyes are wild.

"You?" he growls. "And Whitney?"

There's a faint murmur behind me. I don't know if it's Joaquin or one of the coaches.

I shake my head. "Wyatt's not... you know we're not…"

"You're mine," Sven says, his voice low. His hands settle on my hips, pulling me as close as we can get with the boards in the way. The metal ledge is digging into my belly, but I can't care, because it's keeping me from him.

I swallow.

"Say it," he says. "You're mine."

"I'm yours," I whisper.

Ducking his head, he takes my mouth in a rough kiss. There's nothing sweet or gentle; he attacks my lips, nipping at me. I melt and he draws me closer, half holding me up against the boards as he sweeps his tongue into my mouth.

There's a wolf whistle from behind him. Slowly, Sven pulls away, his eyes glazed.

Grabbing the front of his jersey, I pull him back to me, sliding an arm around his neck to keep him close. His hand dives into my hair, twisting the strands around his fist.

There's a spray of ice, and he jerks back to glare at the interloper.

MacGregor grins, unrepentant. "You realize the broadcast already started, right?"

"So?" He grunts.

"The whole country just saw that kiss. Not the time or place, bud." He claps a hand on Sven's shoulder. "Happy for you two. Would be happier if we got the W tonight, though."

fifteen

· · ·

Sven

WE GET THE WIN. I score two goals and earn an assist on a third.

"Damn, Larsson," Coach Turner says as the clock winds down to the final buzzer. "That's all it took?"

I've been on fire all game. My blood is boiling and my heart is hammering, and it's not from the usual game-time adrenaline.

Vanessa is up in the box. I didn't see her during the two intermissions, laser-focused on the game.

The guys were buzzing, though. Our pre-game kiss was the talk of the arena—and if MacGregor is to be believed, it's headline news.

In the showers, the guys keep trying to tease me, but I keep my head down and focus on getting clean. I'm wrapping a towel around my waist when the locker room door opens and Vanessa, Angelica, and Patrice come inside.

The room gets quiet—quick.

Someone shoves me forward, and I stumble, windmilling my arms. I stop in front of her.

"Hi," Vanessa says, her face red. She tucks some hair behind her ears.

I swallow. "Hi."

"So I guess everyone knows now," she says.

"Yeah."

"Fucking hell," someone says behind me. "This is painful."

"Kiss her, asshole!" someone else shouts.

Vanessa smirks up at me. "You heard him. You gonna kiss me?"

Grabbing her around the waist, I pull her into me, and she smiles as she trails her hands up my arms. She hooks her hands behind my neck, and I lower my lips to hers.

Cheers and whistles erupt behind me.

I don't know what we are now. Are we still faking? Is this real? All I know is that when I saw her hugging Whitney, I couldn't breathe. She's not a possession, she doesn't belong to anyone, but… she's mine. Not his. Even though I know they're friends, even though I know he would never hurt her—

The kiss is much more gentle than pre-game. Coaxing apart the seam of her lips with my own, I tighten my arms around her as she drives her fingers into my hair. I let out a rumbly groan.

"Get a room!" a voice yells.

Suddenly, I remember we're in the middle of the locker room, surrounded by my teammates, and—oh yeah—I'm naked and wearing only a towel.

Vanessa pulls back. "Good game," she says, patting my chest.

"Thanks."

"All right, all right, that's enough," Coach Turner says.

Vanessa pulls away slowly, her eyes on mine as she slides her hand down my arm like she doesn't want to stop touching me. She squeezes my hand before she lets me go.

"Damn," I hear someone say.

When she turns away to go into the back room with Patrice, I shake my head and head back to my locker.

Only—

The guys are staring.

Again.

"What?" I growl out, tired of the silence.

"You and Vanessa Morgan?" McKittrick says, a furrow on his brow.

I nod. "Yeah."

"It was weird that she sat next to you on the plane," Lewis says, looking between me and the back office curiously.

"I saw her coming out of his room in Pittsburgh," Pope chimes in.

Fuckwad.

"So is it, like, a hook up?" Pope continues. "Is she down to fuck?"

White-hot rage burns through me. "Not you."

"They're together," Andrews says from behind me. "Have been for a while."

Over my shoulder, I glare at him. "Stay out of this."

He shrugs. "I've got your back, man."

"So it's true?" MacGregor asks.

"Yeah." Finally reaching my locker, I grab for my clothes. I don't particularly want to drop my towel with a half-chub, but the longer this conversation goes on, the less I'll need to.

"Going after team personnel… that's career suicide, man," Lewis says, shaking his head.

"The team knows. Coach knows. Management knows."

"Really?" I don't understand why Lewis is so surprised.

"As soon as it turned into something, she gave the paperwork to her boss." I shrug. "It's—"

"Hold up." MacGregor sits down. "You filed the relationship form with her?"

I nod. "We weren't hiding anything."

"But you didn't exactly broadcast it, either."

"Because you assholes gossip like schoolchildren." I glare at Pope. "She deserves to be treated with respect. She shouldn't have to have her life be gossip fodder."

"It will be, though," Reynolds points out. "The talking heads asked about it at intermission."

He was interviewed in the break between periods, and I was too in the clouds to notice when he rejoined us.

Fuck.

I blow out a breath. "What did you say?"

He shrugs. "Just that it wasn't my place to comment."

Okay. It could be worse.

I probably should call my agent, though.

"Seriously, man," MacGregor says, nudging me. "Vanessa Morgan? She's, like…"

"Ten out of ten," Cole says.

"Super hot," Reynolds adds.

"Way out of your league," Schwartz says.

At that, I laugh. "Don't I know it."

"Does she have a friend?" Jenkins asks. I can't tell if he's joking, but I'm fairly sure he has a girlfriend.

I lick my lips. "Her best friend is Whitney's little sister."

A few of the guys curse.

Wyatt Whitney is a brawler, unhinged on the best of days. He needled me all game. I didn't even have to be on the ice at the same time to know he was smirking at me.

"Damn it," MacGregor says with a congenial smile. "So she's off limits, then."

"I've always liked a challenge," Pope says, smiling with his teeth.

To my surprise, it's Andrews who pipes up next. "Bex would kick your ass and make you thank her for it."

Pope isn't deterred. "You know her? Is she down to fool around?"

"We went to college together. You touch her, I'll bust your face in, and Whitney can have the leftovers," Andrews says casually as he packs one of the equipment bags. "She's off limits."

"You gonna make a play?" Lewis asks.

Andrews shakes his head. "Nah, it's not that way with us. She's good people, though. Way too good for any of you fuckers."

The guys talk around me. The conversation moves on to what they're doing when we land in Boston.

We've got practice at ten tomorrow morning, so we don't have too much time on the ground to fool around. Some of the younger guys are talking about going out to a bar.

Not me. That wasn't my scene, not even when I was their age, and especially not now.

As I drop my towel in the bin, a big body comes up beside mine.

"Same goes for you, man," Andrews says quietly. "You hurt her, I'll break your face."

"She's not yours," I counter. "She's her own person."

He shrugs. "She's important to me."

"And me, too. Why would I hurt her?"

"Shit happens. I never meant to either, and..." He blows out a breath. "Just... look out for her, okay? What happened with us was ages ago, but that doesn't change the way I feel about her."

I grind my teeth. "Are we going to have problems?"

Andrews blinks. "No, no, not—I don't have *feelings* for her," he stresses. "I respect that you're together. Fuck, you're probably better together than she and I ever were. We weren't suited." He shrugs. "I still care about her. She was a big part of my life."

Mine, too.

It would be so easy to turn the tables around. It could have been me. If I hadn't walked away after that one-night stand eight and a half years ago, would we have made it work? I was already in the league, she was still in school...

When she joined the team, I was in a relationship, and yeah, I ended that quick, but—

Have we just been two sides of the same coin, both wanting her and still wanting her to be happy above all else?

"We're cool, man?" Andrews holds out his hand.

"Yeah, we're cool." I shake his hand.

He claps me on the shoulder. "Go get the girl, Larsson."

sixteen

. . .

Vanessa

ON THE FLIGHT HOME, there's no question: I sit beside Sven.

Immediately after I join row 13, he has his arm around me, pulling me into his side. He presses a light kiss to my temple and I melt into him.

Everyone knows. We don't have to hide.

Although…

We weren't exactly hiding. We were—

I turn my face to his. He's smiling fondly down at me, his expression clear and open.

Leaning up, I press my lips to his, tasting his smile.

The guys around us hoot and holler, and even though my cheeks flame, when Sven holds me close, I can't care about them anymore.

Curling into him, I set my hand on his leg, and I can feel his entire body go tense.

Does he not want me to touch him?

Sven cups my face with his palm, keeping me close. He kisses me softly, sweetly. When he pulls away, he doesn't go far, dropping a soft kiss on my forehead.

He breathes me in, and I take a moment to do the same, memorizing the scent of his soap and his skin.

"Ugh, you guys are so sweet," Jenkins says.

Pope, sitting across the aisle from him, gags. "I might be sick."

Robby, directly behind him, rolls his eyes. "Go be sick somewhere else."

I have to sit in my own seat for takeoff. Sven doesn't go far, though—he holds my hand, running his thumb over the back of my knuckles, and the simple intimacy of it makes my heart sing.

We need to have a conversation.

When we land, I let go of Sven's hand and pull out my phone. It's late, already after midnight, and I'm definitely not taking the T back to my apartment with my luggage.

"What are you doing?" he asks.

I tilt my screen so he can see the rideshare app.

"You're not taking a rideshare at this time of night," Sven says firmly. "I'll drive you."

"But—"

He glares at me.

"Listen to your boyfriend, Van," MacGregor teases. He's sitting behind us, and I glare at him over my shoulder. He smirks as he tucks his phone into his pocket.

It's late, and there's surcharge pricing on the app. With a sigh, I roll my eyes and nod. "Fine. If you insist."

"I do." Sven's quiet determination rings through.

"Nah, man," Robby says. "It's too early to be saying that shit."

Turning to glare at him, he grins and winks at me.

"It's not, though," Sven murmurs, so quiet only I can hear it.

Whipping to face him, his eyes are serious.

"It's not too early."

Laughing nervously, I grab for my purse. We *definitely* need to have a conversation.

His car is a big black SUV with creamy leather seats. He opens the door for me and then stows both his bags and mine in the trunk before rounding to his side.

There's a lemon air freshener on the dash and a Chapstick in the cupholder. When he turns on the ignition, the radio connects to his phone, continuing the audiobook he listened to on the flight. He flicks off the radio.

"Do you want to come to my place?" he asks guilelessly.

"I should go home. It's late."

Sven accepts this at face value, and I punch my address into the car's GPS, even though he dropped me off after our impromptu sleepover.

For a minute there, I was thinking about going home with him. For a minute, I was thinking about more with him.

And those four words? "It's not too early." They ring in my head like a bell: *ding ding ding, pay attention.*

So I am.

What are we?

Is this real, or are we still faking it?

His kisses felt real. The display before the game—that felt real, too. And in the locker room?

The lines are too blurry.

As he pulls up in front of my apartment, Sven cuts the engine.

"We need to talk," I tell him, turning to face him.

He nods. "I scared you."

"Yes." How can I think about forever when I don't even know where we stand?

"I apologize for making you uncomfortable," he says quietly. "I know there's nothing with you and Whitney, you've never made me doubt your integrity. When I saw him with you, I saw red."

In the middle of a nod, I pause. "Wait, what?"

He raises his eyebrows. "When he kissed you?"

I blink a few times. "You think that scared me?"

He nods.

"No, Sven, it didn't scare me," I tell him slowly.

"Then what did?"

"Oh, I don't know, maybe the part when you started talking about 'I do'?"

He swallows. "Oh."

"Yeah." I blow out a breath. "How much of this is real, how much is still a lie?"

"I've never lied to you." His voice is quiet, strong. "The one thing I've never done is lie to you."

"But—"

His hand covers mine on the center console. "I agreed to this because I had feelings for you, feelings I would never act on while you worked for the team. I'm not going to deny them."

"Why?"

"You don't date hockey players," he says simply. "That's your boundary. It would hardly be appropriate for me to try to change your mind."

I stare at him.

"I want you to like me for who I am, not what I can do for you," Sven continues.

"I do. I mean, I do like you," I say awkwardly. "I just…"

He waits patiently.

"Marriage? That's, like…" I laugh nervously.

His dark green eyes meet mine. "I'm following your lead."

It's my turn to swallow. "Wow. So you—"

Squeezing my hand, he shrugs. "It's never been like it was with you with anyone else."

"What do you mean?"

"You're the one I compared everyone else to," he says simply.

I freeze.

"After all, I rather had to. That was my first experience."

I gape at him. "What?"

Sven blinks, cocking his head. "Is this too much?"

"What do you mean, it was your first experience?"

"At Jackson's wedding. The night we were together," he says.

"Yeah. I remember it. We hooked up."

His face tints pink. "You were the first person I ever slept with."

"How?"

"What do you mean, how? You were there. We—"

"I was already twenty, so you would have been nineteen or close to it," I barrel on. "And you were already in the league."

He rolls his eyes. "So?"

"So? I'm sure there were women throwing themselves at you. Hell, I threw myself at you."

"I waited until I was ready," he says simply. "I was a neurodivergent, hockey-obsessed weirdo who had been thrust into the spotlight and barely knew how to talk to my teammates, much less talk to pretty women. I didn't want to get it over with. I wanted to be comfortable with the decision."

"But—if I'd known, I would have…"

He squeezes my hand again. "I didn't want that."

"It should have been… I don't know, special, or memorable, or—"

"It was," he says firmly. "Do you really think I would let myself forget?"

I look away. "I mean, it was just sex."

"No, it wasn't," he says slowly. "We had a connection that night. We still do."

I think back to that night… It's been a long time, but I can't deny it hasn't been on my mind on and off over the years. Especially once I joined the team. But…

"Tell me I'm not alone in this. Tell me I'm not the only one to feel this way," he implores.

"I... I..."

Sven inhales sharply. "I see."

"This is just... a lot," I say lamely. "It's late. A lot has happened today. I just—I need to sleep on this."

"Okay," he says quietly. He opens his door and rounds the SUV to pop the trunk, extracting my suitcase and work bag. I open the car door before he can, reaching for my bags.

"Thanks for the ride home," I tell him.

"Anytime."

He ducks down to kiss me.

I can't.

At the last moment, I turn my face, so he gets my cheek.

"Goodnight, Vanessa," he says quietly.

My eyes well with tears. He sounds so sad. I want to turn around, tell him that I want this, want him, that I—

But I don't.

I can't.

Not while I'm still unsure. He deserves more than my hasty non-confrontational non-truths.

It isn't until I'm in my apartment, changed into my pajamas and climbing into my bed, that the heavy weight of the evening crashes into me.

He likes me.

More than that, he compares other women to me.

Because I was his first.

He's ready to say I do.

He wants this. He wants me.

He—

Curling into a ball, I bury my face in my pillow.

I don't think I can do this.

seventeen

. . .

Sven

BRAD CALLS me at the ungodly hour of eight o'clock in the morning. Normally, that wouldn't be a big deal, except I got home shortly after one o'clock, and then laid in bed until close to four unable to sleep.

Did I fuck everything up?

"You're headline fucking news, bud," Brad says when the line clicks open.

"Okay." What else is there to say? I scrub a hand over my face and sit up.

"Really? You kiss some staffer in front of—"

"She's not some staffer," I interject. "She's my girlfriend."

At least, she was at the time. Now… I'm not so sure.

"You need to be getting along with the team, not causing more drama," he barks.

"I'll take it under advisement."

"I fucking can't with you, bud," he says. "Don't you want this?"

"I do."

I wince at those two little words… fuck.

I scared her. I want her, I'm committed to this, and she's nowhere near ready. Dropping that conversational bomb—on the freaking plane, where others could hear it—really was not my smartest move.

"Fucking act like it," Brad says. "Stop messing around with some puck bunny and—"

"She's not a puck bunny."

"They all are." He scoffs. "Just be glad the last one walked away before you signed over half your assets."

"This conversation has ceased to be productive," I announce. "I'm hanging up now."

He starts to speak.

I stab at my phone until it hangs up the call.

Shit. I haven't thought about Marika in years. Not since I ended things. Last I heard, she was married to another player and living back home in Sweden.

Brad wasn't wrong; it was a good thing Marika and I ended things before the wedding. She didn't put up a fight. She just… left.

Not for the first time, I catalog all the similarities between her and Vanessa. They're both blonde and blue-eyed, and Marika was tall and willowy, but she didn't have Vanessa's spark. She was… flat. She was a perfectly fine person and would have made an excellent hockey wife. I was content to settle with her—until Vanessa walked back into my life.

And the girlfriend before her?

Anja was—well, she was blonde when I met her, and she had light eyes. She pursued me. It didn't last long, maybe a few months at most. Once she dyed her hair to her natural auburn color, I realized I'd been comparing her to Vanessa the whole time. It was hard to stay interested after that.

With Janie, it was all hormones. We only spoke in bed—and we didn't say much. It took six weeks to figure out that physical chemistry aside, I didn't actually like her, and she didn't particularly care for me. She kept calling me Steven, like that would erase my Swedish heritage.

Hookups and casual sex don't do it for me. The lack of

emotional intimacy makes the physical intimacy unfulfilling. I've tried a few times to make it work and I always walk away feeling worse for it. Most of the time, I'd rather take care of my own needs by myself than pretend to be interested in anyone else. Then I'd just be lying and manipulating them into sex, and I don't think I could live with myself if that were the case.

I don't like liars.

I didn't lie to Vanessa. I just... didn't tell her the whole truth. Honestly, if she knew I broke off my engagement because I wanted to be with her, she'd probably run away screaming about stalkers.

Until she came back into my life, I was perfectly content to marry Marika. Maybe not enthusiastic, but it was expected. We were... fine.

And then Vanessa started at the training facility. I made it three days before I told Marika it was over.

It was better to be alone than with the wrong person. I just couldn't see that Marika was the wrong person until the right person showed up right in front of me.

And now I might lose her forever.

Since I have to be at the training facility soon, I might as well get up. After checking on Rupert and my sourdough starter, I pour two travel mugs of coffee, using the last of Brigitte's Oreo creamer in the second cup.

I don't have enough time to bake, so I hit up the cafe on the corner and pick up an assortment of pastries. We've only had two breakfasts together. There aren't enough data points to know what she likes yet. I get two of everything.

She's not at her desk when I get to the back office. Depositing the coffee and the box of pastries on her desk, I head to the locker room, change, and then hit the weights.

The day passes by achingly slow. I can't have my phone on me when I'm on the ice—that's just a recipe for disaster. After my session with the massage therapist, I'm feeling achy and ready to crash. So of course it's when I'm about to head out that Coach calls me into his office.

"You made a spectacle out of that girl," he says when I shut the door.

With a sigh, I scrub my face with my hand. "It won't happen again."

"It won't. The focus should be on the team, not any one individual," he snaps.

"I understand."

"I don't want any funny business," Coach says with a frown. "When we're on the road, you'll each have your own rooms."

"Understood." It's easier than explaining that we aren't sleeping together.

"I expect you to stay in your separate rooms," he continues, as if I haven't spoken. "Nothing happens on the road."

I nod.

"The second she becomes a distraction…"

"I'm on a points streak since we started seeing each other," I tell him honestly. "She gives me something to play for."

He glares at me. "That logo on your chest gives you something to play for."

"It's renewed focus. I'm putting in more effort, paying attention to the small details."

"I thought that was because it's a contract year." He smirks at me.

"She makes me want to stay."

Coach raises his eyebrows.

"Her life is here. I think she wants to stay here." I shrug. "So I'm here as long as she wants to be."

"And if you get traded or sign somewhere else? What, she'll go with you?"

"That's up to her." The thought of leaving while she stays doesn't make me feel good, though.

"So I'll lose a Logistics coordinator, too." He scratches at his beard. "Are you trying to blackmail me? Keep you so we can keep her?"

I shake my head. "Our jobs are irrespective of each other."

"Larsson, you can have your pick of the bunnies. Why her? Why this one?"

"Because she's it for me."

Coach shakes his head. "Better lock it down, then, and get your ring on that girl's finger."

"Trust me, sir," I say with a small smile. "I'm trying."

———

Vanessa is at her desk, her boss standing at the entrance to her cubicle with her arm over the wall. Scott, the third Logistics coordinator, is sitting on his desk so he can be at eye-level with them.

"It was nice of management to bring us pastries," Scott says.

"Yeah. It was," Vanessa says. Her eyes narrow on me.

"Funny how they showed up at your desk," Jacky says casually. She looks in my direction and winks. "Isn't it crazy that there was also a cup of coffee made just the way you like it?"

"Yeah," she says, her voice hollow. "It is crazy."

"Hey, look," Scott says loudly. "Your boyfriend is here."

"Gee, thanks," Vanessa snaps. "I hadn't noticed."

He laughs. "Trouble in paradise already, Van?"

She stands and glares at him. "Shut up." She turns back to me and glares some more. "We need to talk."

Mute, I nod, and she brushes past me, down the hall.

"No hanky-panky in the storage closet," Scott calls after her.

She flips him off.

Pulling me into the copy room, she shuts the door behind her and crosses her arms over her chest.

"You can't do this."

"Do what?" I'm honestly confused by the hostility. "I wanted to check in on you."

"You can't just buy me things and expect—" She lets out a grunt of frustration. "You brought the pastries?"

Nodding, I step toward her, and she flinches back. "I wanted to apologize."

Her eyebrows go up. "For?"

"I threw too much at you," I say simply. "A lot has happened in the last twenty-four hours, and I understand that you need time to process. So—apology pastries."

"You probably bought out the bakery."

Shrugging, I admit, "I wanted to make sure you got your favorites."

Vanessa bites her thumb. "I liked the chocolate croissant."

"I'll bring you one tomorrow."

"No." She sighs. "You shouldn't."

"Why not?" I cock my head.

"You can't love-bomb me and magically I'll—"

"Hold on." I lift my hand. "What is love-bomb?"

I'm pretty fluent in English, they teach us in school from such a young age, but I haven't heard that phrase before.

Her eyebrows knit together. "It's when you go overboard with attention and affection, to the point where you're trying to influence how someone else feels. Usually not for good reasons."

"That's not my intent." I wait until she meets my gaze. "That was not my intent at all. I wanted to do something nice for you."

Vanessa pauses. "I just… it's a lot."

"I know. And that's why I wanted to apologize," I repeat. "It was unfair of me to drop all of that on you, especially in a place where you couldn't get away."

Cornering her in my car… not my brightest move.

"I just... we kissed for the first time yesterday," she says weakly.

Nodding, I agree. "And that was too much? With everyone knowing?"

She shrugs. "It feels like I'm watching someone else live my life instead of me actually getting to experience it. I'm not used to being the center of attention. I don't think I particularly like it."

"Where does that leave us?"

She bites her lip.

"I play hockey. There's a certain level of attention that gets focused on me, whether I like it or not." And ninety-nine percent of the time, I'm firmly in the "not" category.

"I know." Her voice is strained.

Swallowing my fears, I ask, "Do you not date hockey players because of the notoriety?"

"That's part of it." She looks down at her feet. "Robby—he broke my heart. It took me a long time to separate what happened with him and me from everything to do with hockey. It helped to work here, but then I had to keep boundaries because of work. I don't want anyone to think I'm sleeping my way to a promotion."

"He cares about you."

She looks up at me, her eyes wide. "I don't—"

"He told me yesterday, he supports us," I continue. "He cares about you."

Her face twists in an angry scowl. "He can go fuck himself."

Is it normal to have such bitterness over an ex after so many years? I honestly don't know. All of my previous relationships ended amicably. Almost unemotionally.

"Regardless." I clear my throat. "I want you to understand that I'm in this, I'm committed to this. To you."

"We just started... I mean, yesterday was a lot," she says helplessly. "What are we doing?"

"Well, we're dating," I tell her. "Isn't that what you wanted?"

She nods slowly. "Yeah, but you said—"

"I'm ready for something long-term. I'm ready for... everything."

Marriage, kids, forever... I want all of that with her, and more.

Vanessa looks away. "Look, it's..."

"I'm sure about what I want," I tell her. "That's not going to change."

She raises an eyebrow. "It might."

"It won't," I promise.

Vanessa shifts her weight. "Sven..."

"I can wait for you to catch up to me. Just because I'm already there doesn't mean you have to be, too."

After all, I've had the last three and a half years to prepare.

She swallows. "I need some space."

eighteen

. . .

Vanessa

MY EYES ARE red and bloodshot when I get into work the next morning. Jacky takes one look at me and hauls me into her office.

"Do I have to maim somebody?" she demands.

I shake my head. "Only if that somebody is me."

My boss frowns. "Explain."

"I think I broke my own heart."

"I heard about you and Sven on the news," Jacky says carefully. "It's all over social media."

"Yeah, well…" I shrug one shoulder. "Turns out we're in very different places."

Her eyebrows lift. "Oh?"

"I just need some space." My eyes well with tears again. Angrily, I rub them away. "He wants marriage and babies and forever, and I—"

My voice catches.

"Do you not want those things? Or do you want them with someone else?" Jacky asks.

Swallowing the lump in my throat, I admit: "I don't know that I'm cut out for it."

"What makes you say that?"

"My parents split up when I was three years old."

"Okay… lots of people get divorced. It's not the end of the world. I know you probably don't want to think about you and Sven getting divorced, but—"

I shake my head. "I don't know if I even believe in the happily ever after fallacy anymore. I don't get to have that."

"Vanessa…" Jacky reaches for my hand. "You can have that. You can have anything you want."

"The new assistant equipment manager…"

"Did he do something? Do I need to get HR involved?" she demands.

"He… we dated. In college." I rub at my eyes again. "We were together for two and a half years, and we were talking about getting married after I graduated so I could travel with him when he signed with the league."

Jacky watches me, guarded. She lets me take my time to regroup.

"He dumped me. On my twenty-first birthday."

"That cocksucker," she hisses.

I shrug. "Well, yeah. I hadn't talked to him until he started working here. And now every day I have this physical reminder of one of the worst times in my life, and—"

"But you have Sven," Jacky interrupts.

"That doesn't make the pain Robby caused go away. It only compounds it. Because Sven is talking about the same things, but who's to say that whatever I did to make Robby run away won't happen again?"

"Or maybe," she says gently, "It had nothing to do with you."

Wait, what?

"He would have been, what, twenty-one, twenty-two? And about to go into a professional hockey career?" Jacky shakes her head. "That's a lot to deal with. Hell, half of our players can't keep a relationship intact, and of the ones that do, they'll split up two years after retirement."

"See? It's not meant to be."

"I've seen the way he looks at you."

"So?"

"I've never seen a man more in love," Jacky says. "He practically worships the ground you walk on. And this was before anyone knew about you two."

I purse my lips. "I don't think that's true."

"Trust me, it is."

"Whatever."

"The point stands, whatever happens down the line, he's clearly in love with you now. Why are you worried about future pain when you can be happy for now?"

I swallow. "I didn't see it coming last time. I don't want to be caught off guard again."

"Oh, Van…" Jacky squeezes my hand.

"It's okay. I'm fine."

She laughs. "And if you're not, that's fine, too."

"Is there a reason you wanted to talk to me?"

Deflection. It always works, sixty percent of the time.

"I wanted to check in, make sure you're okay," Jacky says.

"I'm fine," I lie again.

She opens her mouth.

"I'd like to get to work, if that's okay. I could use the distraction."

She nods. "Let me know if you need anything. The team will be in soon for film review. If you want to head out early, we can make that happen."

I give her a teary smile. "Thanks. But I don't need that. I'm fine."

Heading back to my desk, I get a look at myself in the reflection of my computer screen. My eyes are red and swollen from crying, my face is splotchy without makeup, and my hair is stringy and greasy because I didn't have the energy to wash it. No wonder Jacky was worried.

Still, I have work to do, so I put my head down and get to work. I need the distraction.

About an hour in, a delivery arrives, and Jacky sets a small bag on my desk.

"What's this?"

She shrugs. "It says Vanessa Morgan on the note."

It's a small brown paper bag from a bakery in Beacon Hill. Intrigued, I open it to find two perfect chocolate croissants and a small folded note.

V— Take all the time you need. I'll be here when you're ready.

Though it's not signed, I know exactly who it's from.

———

The last thing I expect is for Robby fucking Andrews to come to my desk. What the hell kind of game is he playing? Can't I get a freaking moment of peace from the memory of that douchebag without having to see his fucking face?

Robby is wearing a team staff t-shirt and athletic pants. He moves stiffly, and for a brief moment, I feel a flicker of concern before I lock it away. Is he hurt? Did he aggravate his knee injury?

I shouldn't care about him. He's nothing to me.

But…

We were close once. At one time, I thought he was my forever.

"Hi, Nessie," Robby says. He puts his arm over the top of my cubicle, and his familiar scent wafts toward me. "Can we talk?"

"Why? There's nothing to talk about." I keep my focus on my computer screen, even though I haven't been able to pay attention since he walked into the back office two minutes ago.

"I'd like to buy you a cup of coffee," he says. He clears his throat. "Off site, if that's possible."

"I'd really rather not."

"We need to talk," he says firmly. "Clear the air."

"There's nothing to clear."

He sighs. "Nessie…"

I flinch. "Don't call me that."

"You never used to mind."

"Yeah, well, a lot has changed."

"I suppose so." He coughs. "Please. I'll stop, I'll leave you alone. I just really think we need to talk."

My stomach twists. The last thing I want is to relive those memories again and again.

"What do you want to talk about? You dumped me in college, I have a new boyfriend now, and I'm happy. Why the fuck do you think I still think about you?"

Shit. I wasn't supposed to say that.

Because I do. All the fucking time. Not in an "I miss him" kind of way, but in a "why the hell am I so unlovable?" doubt spiral.

I mean, Bex and Elsy love me. Wyatt is practically my brother, too. I might even buy that Sven loves me, misguided as he may be.

Since Robby broke up with me on my birthday, I haven't had a relationship that lasted more than one night. My friends are supportive and always there for me. I don't need anyone else.

Except…

"Please," Robby says quietly. "I'd really like to talk to you."

"Ugh. Fine." I power down my computer and lean into the aisle. "Jacky, I'm headed out."

"Good. Don't forget you have the next few days off, too," she says from her open office.

Wait. What? That's news to me.

"But—"

"We have a three-game homestead. Scott is on shift, and I'll be backup. Enjoy the time off, because when you get back, you're on the road out to Austin and New Orleans."

"Okay. Thanks, I guess."

Shoving my stuff into my work bag, my eyes fall to the bakery bag. I devoured those chocolate croissants, but the note is still on the corner of my desk.

He'll give me the space I need. Great. Fine.

So why do I feel so hollow?

Robby jerks his head toward the elevator, and dutifully I follow him.

"Why off site?" I ask as he punches the button for the ground floor.

He shakes his head. "Contrary to popular belief, I don't actually want my personal life to be gossip fodder," he says.

I snort.

"Also, I think it would be better if we can't be overheard or interrupted, and we might need some privacy."

"Privacy? For what? Do you seriously think I'm going to screw you for old times' sake?"

He scoffs. "Trust me, Nessie, that's not what I'm after."

My hands on my hips, I turn to him. "Excuse me?"

He opens his mouth to argue, then stops. "Let's get some coffee and chat."

There's a cafe across the street, and we walk in silence out of the training facility and down the street. It's chilly out, and I pull my coat tighter around me like I can magically wring out more warmth from the fabric.

At the coffee shop, I order a latte and Robby gets a green

tea before he heads toward the comfortable armchairs by the window.

He opens his mouth, then pauses. Starts again, then stops.

"Spit it out," I snap. "I don't have time for this."

Robby sighs. "What I'm going to tell you—this is in no way your fault, and it has nothing to do with you. I just think you deserve an explanation."

My eyes narrow. "Excuse me?"

His eyes flick to mine. "I'm gay."

Uh… what?

"I'm gay," he repeats. "I'm out to friends and family, but not in the league, so I'd appreciate it if you didn't spread it around quite yet."

"But—we—"

"I didn't know until after we broke up," he rushes to admit.

I cross my arms. "Yeah. You want to talk about that? On my fucking birthday?"

He winces. "I was a dick."

"Yeah, you were, fuckhead," I snap.

Robby shakes his head. "I deserve that. I do."

His words echo in my head. He's gay. He's not interested in me. Maybe he never really was.

"So what was I? Just a beard?"

"No. Not at all." He sips from his tea, scratching at his jaw. "A few weeks before… everything, we went to dinner with my parents. Remember?"

I do. They asked about my intentions with their son and our future relationship plans, most likely to find out if I was a gold digging whore or if I actually had feelings for him. His parents were not kind to me when we got together, and they didn't warm up to me over the two and a half years we were together. They didn't like the idea of me with their son, holding him back from the sport he loved for the sake of my love for him.

Because I did. I loved him.

Past tense. Loved.

"You told them we wanted to get married."

He winces. "I did, yeah."

"So what changed?" I demand.

"My mom offered me her diamond ring, and I... well, I freaked out," he admits. "I couldn't handle the pressure of getting married. It was overwhelming. Especially with the league looming over me." He blows out a breath. "For two weeks, I convinced myself it was just cold feet. I planned this perfect proposal."

My eyes widen. "What?"

"I planned to propose on your birthday," Robby blurts.

"And instead you dumped me." My voice is hard. My heart is harder.

"I thought it was just the idea of marriage in general," he continues. "It took me about a year to realize it was the thought of marrying a woman that terrified me."

My eyebrows go up.

"I never really... I wasn't interested in guys, or so I thought. I admired them, and I looked up to them, but I never wanted to fool around with them. And everyone looks in the locker room, even if they say they don't." He blushes. "I... well, I had this teammate, and we... well, I figured out pretty quickly that I was into dudes, and after a bit of soul-searching, I put the pieces together."

"But we... I mean, you and I..." I wave my hands.

"We had sex. We had a lot of sex," he says bluntly.

"Yeah. That."

"All I knew was something wasn't right, but I didn't know what it was," Robby says.

"So you're gay? You're not bi?"

He blows out a breath. "I had those two girlfriends in high school, and you and I were together, but I wasn't... women never caught my eye the same way. And now that I've been with a few men, I can see the absence of a real connection with anyone previous."

I swallow. "Is this because of me? Because of something I did?"

"Nessie, no. No, no." He reaches for my hand, and to my surprise, I let him take it. "I've always been gay, I just didn't know it yet. It has absolutely nothing to do with you."

"But—"

"I was born this way. I always have been, and always will be gay, and there's nothing anyone can do to change that." He shakes his head. "It's not a bad thing. It's kind of a relief, really, to figure out this part of me that was missing for so long."

My throat is dry, and I take a sip of my latte, but it's too hot and it burns my tongue.

"Larsson is a good guy," Robby says, shifting the subject.

I look away. "I don't want to talk about him."

"He and I had a chat the other day, and it made me realize you needed to know my truth," he continues. "I don't have romantic feelings for you, but a part of me will always love you, and now that I have you back in my life, I don't want to lose you again."

My stomach lurches. "Uh, what?"

"We were good together. As a couple, yeah, we had our faults. But if I were attracted to women, you'd be everything I'd want. Fuck, you *were* everything I wanted."

"But that changed."

"But I realized what I needed in a partner," he corrects. "And it has absolutely nothing to do with you or anything you did, it was all me. It just took me some time to figure it all out."

"So… what now?"

"Larsson loves you," he says.

I roll my eyes and look away.

"He loves you, and I saw the look on your face when he started talking about marriage on the plane last night."

"Yeah. You're the one that brought it up."

"That was meant to be a teasing joke," he says, like that absolves him. "I honestly intended it to be a lighthearted comment until he made it all serious." He squeezes my hand, and I start, because I hadn't realized he was still holding it. "Nessie, you are incredibly important to me, and a part of me will always love you."

I choke.

"I don't have romantic feelings for you, I don't want to break up your relationship, I don't want to win you back. I just want you to not hate me."

Staring out the cafe window, I try to recalibrate.

Because he's right. I did hate him. I do hate him. It's been years, but I'm still carrying around the fresh hurt of a broken heart all the fucking time, and nothing I've ever been able to do has taped it back together again.

"I'm in Boston for the long term," Robby continues. "Hopefully, at least. I like the team. I want to stay here. But if you want me gone, at the end of the season, I'll put in applications with the league. I can—"

"You don't have to leave."

The words come out before I realize I spoke them.

Clearing my throat, I continue. "You don't have to leave on account of me, at least."

"Nessie…"

"I don't know that I can forget what happened," I tell him slowly. "But eventually, I think I'll be able to find a way to forgive you."

Not today. Maybe not tomorrow. But hopefully, it will be sometime soon.

"Larsson loves you," he says again. "He's serious about you. I just didn't want to be the reason that you keep him at arm's length."

I open my mouth.

"I know you, Nessie. He blindsided you last night."

Quietly, I nod. "I wasn't expecting it."

"I hope we can be friends again," Robby says. "I really want us to be friends. Whatever that looks like. I just want you in my life."

Swallowing my fears, I meet his eyes. "We might be able to make that happen."

nineteen

. . .

Sven

I'VE FUCKED EVERYTHING UP.

Case in point: my sourdough starter was left out a little too long in the direct path of a sunbeam, and it burst the glass jar holding it captive.

Also: Rupert hasn't said "good girl" to me in the four days I've been home. I think she's upset with me for leaving her with Brigitte, even though my bird-sitter is always coming in and cleaning even during the offseason.

Oh yes: And Brad keeps texting me, threatening me and insulting me in the same message. If it wasn't such a pain to find a new agent and train them to deal with me, I might switch. But I don't have the patience or the time for that.

All of this is eclipsed, of course, by the fact that I haven't talked to Vanessa in way too long. She hasn't called or texted or emailed or sent a carrier pigeon since I sent her the note about giving her space. How much damn space does she need, an entire fucking planet?

Blowing out a breath, I knead the bread dough with all of my frustration. It's not her fault that we're in different places. Genuinely, I am fine with giving her space. I just don't like the silence.

I guess now I know how she felt at the beginning when I wasn't texting her back.

What the hell am I supposed to do now?

When my bread comes out of the oven, I package it and head across the street. Hildy opens the door right away, pulling me into the house by the front of my sweatshirt.

"You have been avoiding me," she scolds.

"I've been busy," I deflect.

"You have never been too busy for me."

With a sigh, I hold out the bread. "It's complicated. Do you have time for some tea?"

She scowls. "If you insist."

As she fills the kettle and pulls two mugs out of the cabinet, she waves her hand toward the bread box, where a loaf of seeded pumpernickel is waiting.

"Make a sandwich," she says. "You look hungry."

Shaking my head, I do as she says, pulling out butter, sliced meat, and cheese. I'm used to this. She's been feeding me since the moment we met when I bought the place. I'm not sure how or why she realized I was starving for more than simple human contact. Though she's from Germany where I am Swedish, we both understand how it is to be a foreigner in a new country, adapting to everything new at once. She's my home, in a way the building I live in is just a house. I'll surely miss her when I have to leave Boston, whenever that may be.

As she requested, I make a sandwich. And then I make a second, and a third, until we have a plate full of open-faced sandwiches on freshly sliced bread.

"Is Brigitte here?" I ask as the kettle whistles, and she pulls it off the stove. I bring the two cups to the table, and she brings the kettle, pouring water.

Hildy shakes her head. "She's at the university."

Her niece is in her final year of medical school, and in her spare time, she comes across the street to take care of Rupert.

When Hildy realized I needed a bird watcher, she organized for Brigitte to stay at my place across the street and take care of my bird—and the house—while I was out.

"Did you call her?" Hildy asks, and it takes me a second to realize she means Brigitte.

"No. Should I?"

"Aren't you looking for her?"

I shake my head. "I thought I might need a woman's perspective."

"Oh?" Her eyebrows go up. "On what?"

"How to make Vanessa not need more space."

She pauses. "And who is Vanessa?"

"My girlfriend?" I think she still is, at least…

She frowns.

"What?"

"I rather thought…" She trails off.

"Tell me."

"I always thought one day you and Brigitte would…" She waves her hands. "You two could…"

I blink. "We would what?"

Hildy sighs. "That you two would date."

My eyes widen. "Me? And Brigitte?"

"Yes." She stirs more sugar into her tea. "I had hopes… but you never seemed to act upon it."

"Brigitte is your niece." My whole body feels numb. How could she ever think I would be remotely interested in crossing that boundary?

"I am aware," she says dryly.

"And my employee."

She pauses. "I wasn't aware that is how you viewed her."

"How else am I supposed to view her?" I'm genuinely curious. It never occurred to me to see her as anything other than my employee.

"She's your age, she's single, she's pretty…"

My mind gets stuck. "But she works for me."

"I know."

"And she's your niece."

"Yes," Hildy says, sipping her tea. "I didn't realize that was such a problem for you."

"It's not. It wouldn't be. It—fuck." I scrub at my forehead. "I would not date your niece without consulting you first, and I would not consult you about your niece unless I were interested in seriously pursuing her. And the fact remains, I am only interested in seriously pursuing Vanessa—the same woman I've been interested in for several years now."

She presses her lips together. "Is she that woman who came here a few nights ago?"

"It was a few weeks, and yes. We are dating." It feels stiff and formal for our relationship. "We're together," I try again. "Well—I want to be, I may have messed everything up. Which is why I wanted to talk to Brigitte," I add. "I was hoping she had some insight as to where I went wrong."

"Did you apologize?" Hildy asks dryly.

I nod. "I sent her an apology gift and a note. That was a few days ago."

"What did you do prior to that?"

"I... well, I told her I was interested in getting married, and she was not expecting that," I finally explain.

"Have you been dating long?"

"Not terribly long, no." With a sigh, I lift my tea, then set it down without drinking. "That may be part of the problem."

She gives me a cold look that tells me in no uncertain terms that I'm a fucking idiot. "Perhaps."

"So... what do I do about it?"

"Well, you could give her time to acclimate and decide if she feels the same," Hildy offers.

"Or?"

"Or, you could force the issue and make her resent you more," she continues. "Possibly ending it altogether."

Ending it? My blood runs cold at the thought. I have

waited all this time to get Vanessa back into my life—I don't think I could stand it if she were to leave me now.

"I don't like that." I don't want to force her into anything.

"Well…"

"Thank you," I tell my friend and neighbor. "I needed a woman's perspective."

She shakes her head. "I think you knew what to do all along. You just did not want to admit it."

twenty

. . .

Vanessa

I WOULD LIKE to say that I spent my time off being productive… but instead, I was a potato. I sat on the couch and watched Real Housewives of wherever for hours until my ass got numb, and then I moved to my bed and watched a few more episodes, and then I fell asleep… and when I woke up, I moved back to the couch and started all over again.

Things I did not do in my three days off:
1. *Laundry*
2. *Dishes*
3. *Wash my hair*

Things I did:
1. *Approximately nothing*
2. *Eat my weight in raw cookie dough*
3. *Obsess over my conversation with Robby*

I'm on day two of potato-ing when Elsy gets home from work, sees me, and sighs.

"Oh, honey," she says, shaking her head. "This is not what we do."

"Yeah, it is." I pick out another pre-portioned glob of ready-to-bake cookie dough.

"I gave you some time, but this—it's too much." She takes a seat on the other couch, across from mine. "Are you ready to talk about it?"

"He's gay," I say bluntly.

Her eyebrows go up. "Sven?"

"What? No. Robby."

She pauses. "Robby, as in… your college boyfriend?"

I nod.

"The one who works with you?"

Again, I nod.

"Why do we care about Robby? In this context? Aren't you happy with Sven? He kissed you on national television!" She smiles, like I should be happy about that.

"Yeah, and then two hours later, he said he wanted to marry me," I tell her bitterly.

Elsy freezes. "Um… what?"

"The last guy who talked about marriage dumped me on my fucking birthday, and now he tells me he planned to propose that night, but I'm just so unloveable he decided he —" I hiccup. "He's gay. And we were together for two and a half years. What does that say about us?"

Elsy sighs. "Okay, let's back up a second. Sven said he wants to marry you?"

I nod. "And when we talked about it the next day, he doubled down and said it again. Fuck." Rubbing at my eyes, I blink away the tears before she can spot them. "So clearly I am an excellent judge of character."

"Yeah, you are," she says, ignoring my sarcasm. "What does all this have to do with Robby?"

"He cornered me a few days ago, and he came out to me."

On the one hand, a part of me does feel gratified that he trusts me enough to share his truth with me, but a bigger piece of me is still reeling from reliving those old memories and hurts.

I thought I had moved on. I was fine. Instead, I think I was really just repressing everything, pretending everything was okay.

I never dealt with it. I've been avoiding romantic relationships for years, sticking instead to brief sexual encounters to scratch the itch, and obtaining my need for companionship with a lively group of friends who love me unconditionally.

Because I thought Robby did. Love me unconditionally, that is.

"Sometimes we don't know what's missing until we find it," Elsy says slowly. "It's like—when I'm composing, I can hear it in my head, but I can't always separate each instrument with each note until I really start looking for it."

"I don't follow."

"His being attracted to men has nothing to do with the time he spent with you," she says. "Dating is like... like picking locks. You have an infinite number of keys, and you don't know which one will be the right fit, but you keep trying. Because that's what you have to do—you keep trying. And sometimes it's not a perfect fit, but it works well enough that you can jimmy it open, at least for now."

Scooping out another glob of cookie dough, I consider this.

"And then it turns out that instead of being one key for each lock, there are multiple keys. So the first worked for a while until it got sticky, so you try something new, and when you find the next... you might not be looking for it or expecting it to work, but when you try it, it just... fits. And you... maybe you don't forget the first key, but you know this second one fits better. It doesn't invalidate everything you had with the first key. It worked for a while, until it didn't. This new key, though? It fits like a glove."

She smirks at me. "Or, alternatively, like a condom, snug and tight."

I roll my eyes.

"Nothing will change the way that he felt about you back then. I know we didn't know each other yet, but I've heard the stories and I've seen the photos. He adored you," Elsy continues. "He just found out something new about himself. It's not like he purposely led you on or hid it while you were together. He found out something new. That doesn't make him a bad person. That makes him human."

"No, no, I know," I tell her. "I just… We were talking about getting married. We were talking about forever. And then he decided…"

She shakes her head. "He didn't decide to be gay. It doesn't work like that."

I sigh. "I know. But—"

"He made a dick move when he broke up with you," Elsy says. "That doesn't make him evil. It makes him human."

"So what do I do?" I hate how helpless I sound. How helpless I feel.

"You forgive him," she says, like it's that easy. "And then you don't punish Sven, or the next one, for something that Robby did. You heal."

"Okay…" I pause. "So, the second part of this issue is— how do I tell my maybe-not fake boyfriend that I like him, but I don't know if I can marry him?"

Elsy blinks. "You… tell him that. With words."

"But, like… how?"

She shakes her head. "We can't do this right now."

"We can't?"

"You need to get up, put away the cookie dough, and take a shower," she announces. "I'll call the girls. We need a club meeting, stat."

twenty-one

. . .

Vanessa

AN HOUR AND A HALF LATER, I'm surrounded by my friends at our favorite local dive bar, and—well, all is not right in the world, but it's slowly getting there.

I think.

Maybe.

Possibly.

"What the hell," Ceci says.

I nod emphatically. "I know, right?"

"Let me get this straight," she says, holding her hand out as if that's going to steady her, when she's already two drinks past tipsy and it's only happy hour. "You have a hot, Swedish hockey player who wants to kiss on you and make sweet, sexy love to you—and instead you're out with us?"

I blink. "Did you not hear a word I just said?"

"I heard you," Arielle says. "I agree with Ceci, though. I think you should get back on that dick."

"Uh… how?" Are we even having the same conversation?

"Love. Angel. Sweetheart," Sadie says. "Butterfly, I love you. You know I do. But I swear to fucking high heaven, if you have the opportunity to get laid and don't take it, I will never forgive you."

Lifting my drink to my lips, I laugh nervously. "You guys are really invested in the state of my vagina."

"Well, babes, it's been a while," Bex points out.

I glare at her. "Thanks, I hadn't noticed," I say tightly.

When Elsy called a meeting of the minds, I didn't expect to be ganged up on. Bex, Ceci, Elsy, and Sadie are all single; only Arielle and Johanna are in relationships, and they're both engaged to awesome guys, so their opinions don't really count.

"This is not the type of gang bang I like," I mutter under my breath, and Johanna winks at me.

"We care about you," Ceci says seriously. "You deserve a chance to be happy."

"Did you not hear the part where he said he wants to marry me?" My voice goes up in volume as it increases in pitch, and people at neighboring tables turn to look at us.

"Yeah, but are you opposed to the idea of marriage in general, or the idea of marrying someone you haven't really been dating?" Johanna asks. "Because Sullivan and I started talking about getting married within the first three weeks, but—"

"You guys were already living together," Arielle points out. "Asher was always upfront that it was what he wanted. We're only waiting until we're both comfortable with the relationship before we spring it on our families."

"Okay, you've known him for twenty years," Sadie adds. They're childhood friends and grew up together, even if they weren't close back then.

Bex leans back in her seat, sipping her drink. "Fuck, just once I'd like the guy to fall first instead of me falling head over tits for an idiot. Do you guys have magic pussy or what?"

Arielle and Johanna glance at each other and grin.

"I have no idea what it is," I tell her honestly. "It's been almost ten years, and—"

Bex rolls her eyes. "One, Katie and Alex got married nine years ago, and—"

I open my mouth to interrupt.

"—and two, he obviously remembers you fondly," she says loudly, over me, "so clearly you did something right."

My memory is hazy on the best of days, least of all with the time elapsed and alcohol consumed between now and then.

"I mean… it was just sex." I shrug helplessly. "We hooked up. We had a good time."

"Did he get you to come, or did you have to do the work yourself?" Sadie asks, raising her eyebrows.

My eyebrows knit together. "It—we—" My face flames, but these women and I are open about pretty much everything. "It took some time. He lacked… finesse."

"But if that was his first time," Ceci says insistently, "and he still managed it? Think what he could do if he actually knew what he was doing."

"I shouldn't have told you that." I bury my face in my hands. "What would you do if a random one-night stand from a decade ago suddenly announced he wanted to marry you?"

She scoffs. Her ex-husband is a piece of work. "Well, we all know that ain't happening, so…"

"Indulge me. Humor me." I stare her down.

"Okay," she allows, "the marriage part is a little much."

"I was still coming around to dating for real instead of dating for pretend," I admit. "And then he throws this curveball at me and I…" I exhale shakily.

"So let's reframe this," Bex says seriously. "Question one: do you like him?"

I swallow. "I like him."

"Question two: do you want to date him?" Sadie joins in.

"Um… I like kissing him," I allow. "And I like his bird. His house is pretty cool, too."

Arielle rolls her eyes. "Dating someone is about more than physicality and possessions. Do you like being around him? Does he make you smile? Laugh? Does he make you feel safe?"

"Well, yeah." I sip my drink. "But marriage…"

"Take marriage off the table," Bex repeats. "Do you want to date him? Yes or no?"

"I—I—"

Sadie shakes her head. "The real question is, do you want to fuck him?"

"Yes."

The word slips out immediately, and I flush, covering my face in my hands.

"So your pussy isn't dead," Johanna says. "Just hibernating."

"Definitely not dead." I think back to how it felt at the game, how everything just melted away until it was him and me and the most perfect kiss. My body warms and I bite my lip, thinking of his growly demands.

"I think you have to go for it," Ceci says. "You'll kick yourself otherwise."

"But—"

Bex rolls her eyes. "For fuck's sake, Vanessa. We're saying to screw the guy, not marry him! You deserve to get laid."

"I don't want to hurt him, though."

"So don't," Sadie says, like it's that simple.

"If he wants more—"

"He's a big boy, he can handle it," she says. "It's up to him to decide if he can handle sex without feelings, just like you have to decide if you want sex with feelings. Except he's not sitting here blathering on about it, he's living his life."

"He isn't, though," I say quietly.

Sadie's eyebrows go up.

"He doesn't go out. He doesn't hang out with the team.

On the road trip, he was watching a movie alone in his room until I interrupted him. He never goes out."

"Maybe he needs an excuse to go out more," Bex says. She nods to Arielle and Johanna. "They're always calling us their social buffers, their reason to get out of the house."

It hits me suddenly. I sit up straight in my seat.

Arielle and Johanna—they're both on the spectrum.

So is Sven.

"What is it?" Arielle asks.

"You two have a lot in common with him," I finally say. It's not my place to go on about his private medical history, especially not things the public isn't entitled to know.

Johanna smirks. "Well, it's called neurospicy for a reason."

"Do you want us to have a double—well, triple date?" Arielle asks. "You already know Asher and Sully. We can get together and prove it's possible for a neurodivergent and neurotypical person to have a functional relationship."

"I know you can. It's not about that." I rub at my forehead. "It's just..."

Bex reaches across the table for my hand. "You're in charge here, Van. He'll have to adapt to your timeline. You can think about what you want. But you need to be sure."

twenty-two

. . .

Sven

GIVING Vanessa space may be the hardest fucking thing I've ever done. We go on a road trip and she sits with the other staffers at the back of the plane, and she doesn't so much as look at me during meals, and—

Pope notices. Other guys do, too, I'm sure. It's just that Pope is the only one to say anything about it.

"Trouble in paradise?" He mocks as we get ready for practice on the third day of our road trip.

I'm going to beat his face in.

"Easy," MacGregor says quietly. "He's not worth getting suspended over."

On that we can agree, at least.

From a distance, I watch—and as I watch her, I see Andrews watching her, too. And she's looking back at him.

Does she want him back? Would she rather be with him than with me?

I respect that he doesn't have feelings for her. But that doesn't mean she feels the same way. She was so broken up over him, going so far as to concoct this insane plot when he first joined the team, and again last week when we talked after the kiss; she acted like they'd broken up last week rather than years ago. People aren't that broken up over someone they don't have feelings for. There is a part of her that still has feelings for him, whether she knows it or not.

So I guess the question is, what do I do about it?

When the plane lands later that night in Boston, I'm exhausted from the travel and the intensity of the game. The only thing I want to do is curl up in my bed and crash. As I fish my car keys out of my bag, I see my teammates headed for their cars, intent on heading home.

Vanessa lingers on the tarmac, her scarf blowing in the wind. Her blonde hair is loose, whipping around her in a maelstrom of waves. She looks like an angel, a sea of yellow and gold nestled amongst the darkness of the night.

"You okay, Nessie?" Andrews shouts to be heard, stopping in front of her.

Our eyes meet.

"I'm good, thanks," she says, giving him a smile.

Andrews looks back at me over his shoulder, and I nod in passing. He tips his chin.

"I'm here if you need anything. K?" He sets his hand on her shoulder.

My blood boils over. That motherfucker. Is he trying to steal her out from under me? I'm going to—

"Thanks, Robby," she says. "I'll be fine."

Her eyes flick to mine.

"Do you need a ride home?" I ask lightly, half expecting her to tell me to fuck off and leave her alone.

"I'd love that, thanks," Vanessa says in that same light tone, like it hasn't been a week since she said she needed space and we haven't talked since.

I take her small wheeled suitcase from her hand, rolling it over to my car as she and Andrews exchange another few words before she jogs after me, falling into step beside me.

"Hi," she says.

Glancing down at her from the corner of my eye, I see her smile and then hide it.

"Hi?"

"We should talk," she says. She bites her lip. "Um…"

As we reach the car, I open her door, then haul the bags into the trunk and get in on my side, automatically cranking the heat and her seat warmer.

She's going to break up with me. She doesn't want to do this anymore. She wants to get back with Andrews. She's—

"Sven, I…" She stops, looking down at her hands.

"I don't want to break up," I blurt.

She blinks. "Um…"

"I gave you space. I gave you time to get acclimated," I push on. "I don't want to break up. However the fuck this started, I'm in this, and you don't get to avoid me for a week and a half and then dump me in a fucking parking lot."

Vanessa clears her throat. "I wasn't breaking up with you," she says quietly.

"What?"

"I wasn't planning on it," she says.

"Isn't that what 'we need to talk' means? I know I don't always pick up social cues, but—"

She shakes her head. "I just… I needed some space to regroup, to think about what I want outside of what I want for you and for us."

"And?"

"And I found out some things, and I've done a lot of soul searching, and… well, breaking up is the last thing I want," she says. "I'm not ready for marriage, I don't really even want to consider it right now. It should be out of the equation."

"Okay…"

"I'm okay with causal. I'm even okay with feelings. I just can't think about forever, at least not yet." Vanessa's eyes meet mine, hesitant. "I like you. I do. And I'm working on my shit. Robby and I—we talked, and I'm working on it," she says. "I just know I'm not in a place yet where I can think about forever. I want to. It's just not something I can do right now."

It feels like I've been punched in the solar plexus. The breath has been knocked out of me, but I can keep going.

"That's okay. We don't need to…"

"I want to date," Vanessa declares. She gestures between us. "We went from zero to sixty and then to a hundred in the blink of an eye. I want to pause. I want dates. I want to get to know you, the person, and not just as the hot hockey player. We need to get to know each other."

"I agree," I tell her evenly.

She pauses. "You do?"

"Yes. We don't have a game tomorrow. Can I take you out?"

To my surprise, Vanessa smiles. "I'd like that. I'd like that a lot."

My answering smile stretches from ear to ear.

"Excellent." I shift the car into gear. "It is a date."

———

When I pull up in front of Vanessa's apartment in Cambridge the next night, I'm a bundle of nerves. It has been a long time since I've been out romantically with a woman, and even longer since I cared about dating.

She's right. We should have been doing this all along.

She lives in a newer building in the trendy part of Cambridge, on the sixth floor of a seven-story building. Taking the elevator up, I knock on the door of number 613 and wipe my sweaty palms on my coat.

The door swings open almost immediately, revealing a tall, curvy redhead wearing a Philly team sweatshirt.

Right. This must be Whitney's sister.

"Hey, I'm Bex," she says, holding out her hand, and it

takes me a minute to realize she wants to shake mine. "You must be Sven."

Clearing my throat, I nod. "Yes. Hi. We—You were at Jackson's wedding. Nine years ago."

Surprise sketches over her features. "Yes. You and Vanessa… well, I'm sure you remember, considering you're together now," she says with an awkward laugh. "Come in. She's almost ready."

The apartment is light and airy, bright with white walls covered in framed prints, watercolors and acrylics. There's a squishy yellow couch and a vibrant forest green armchair, and the small dining table is covered in baby blue enamel.

Shifting my weight, I move the bouquet of winter roses from one hand to the other. "I—um—"

"Oh, those are gorgeous," Bex says, spotting the flowers. "She's going to love them."

I let out a soft sigh. Good. I rather hoped so.

The front door bangs open, followed by a litany of curses.

"Motherfucking asshole fucker fucking bullshit," comes from the mouth of a brunette that looks like she could be Bex's sister – except for the hair.

"You okay, babe?" Bex asks.

"Mitch is a fucking asshole," the woman snarls. "He—" She stops in her tracks. "You're Sven. You play for Boston."

Guarded, I nod.

"Hi. I'm Elsy. I'm Van's roommate. My best friend Mitch plays for New Orleans," she says, like that's an explanation.

I do recall Vanessa mentioning her friend being connected to a hockey player, though…

"What did Mitch do now?" Bex asks soothingly.

"The fucker went and caught that stupid stomach flu that's been going around," Elsy groans. "Now he won't be on the road trip to Boston this weekend."

That's right. We're playing New Orleans on Sunday.

"So you don't get to see your bestie." Bex nods. "That does suck. He is an asshole for that." She winks at me.

"Why don't you go to him?" I ask, before I can think better of it.

Elsy tilts her head at me. "What do you mean?"

"He's sick, he can't travel, so go to New Orleans to see him instead," I tell her.

"I've got work," she says. "And also, gross, I don't want his germs."

"True. Stay far away, don't bring that nonsense back here," Bex grins.

"He's my best friend, we're not dating," Elsy says with a kind smile. "I only get to see him once or twice a year because his offseason is my busy season at the symphony. This weekend was supposed to be my chance. I've only seen him once since I moved to Boston a year and a half ago."

"That must be hard," I comment hollowly, mentally calculating how long it's been since I saw my parents.

It's been about a year and a half for me as well. Longer since I've seen any of my siblings. I know they've been stateside in the last few years for conferences and work obligations, but they haven't called me up once. Then again, the United States is quite different in size from Sweden, and I travel so frequently...

A door snicks open, and my heart pounds as I hear footsteps down the hallway.

"Hey, have you seen—"

Vanessa stops in her tracks.

Her mouth drops open.

"Hi," I say, like an absolute fucking idiot.

"Hi," she whispers.

She looks like she could be on the cover of a fashion magazine. Her hair is down in loose blonde waves, makeup making her face intense and dramatic while still looking like herself. She's wearing a long-sleeved lavender dress that skims a few inches above her knees, dark tights, and silvery pumps with a delicate strap around her ankle. The dress's neckline is fitted to her collarbone, but when she turns, I see the back dips low to her mid back, and my heart thumps at the sight of her smooth, creamy skin on display.

My mouth dries suddenly, and I swallow and lick my lips. "You… you look… Wow."

A flush spreads over her face. "You like?" Vanessa asks, lifting the hem of her skirt and twirling, showing me the back of her dress again. There's a little strap connecting the sides of the dress, a simple string so innocent I could probably rip it with my teeth.

I want to.

Need floods my body, overriding my senses. I want to pull her into my arms and kiss her senseless, but my feet are rooted to the spot. I've had feelings for her for a long time. I've seen her nearly every day for the last four years. But I haven't needed her like I need her now, like my very breath has been stolen and won't be returned until she bestows it upon me.

Nodding emphatically several times until I'm sure I look like a bobblehead toy, I hope to convey what my words can't.

"Yes. Very much. Yes."

Vanessa makes her way over to me, and as I reach for her, I find the flowers in my hand.

"For you," I tell her, handing over the bouquet.

"They're lovely," she says, taking the cellophane-wrapped bundle and bringing it to her nose to inhale the roses' scent.

The sound of the plastic wrapper makes me cringe a little inside—it is not my favorite sound, it is right on the list with styrofoam and cardboard scrapes of DO NOT LIKE—but I do my best to hide my reaction.

She pauses, adjusting her grip and making the plastic rustle more, and I die a little.

"What's wrong?" Vanessa asks.

My shoulders go up around my ears and I shake my head several times. "Nothing."

"Something is wrong."

"The—I don't like the noise. The crinkles." I give a whole body shiver. "It's not a good noise."

"Here, I'll take that," Bex cuts in. I almost forgot she and Elsy were still there. "We'll get rid of the cellophane and put the flowers in water for you."

Robotically, Vanessa hands over the bouquet, and I do my best to block out the sound of the crinkling plastic as it shifts hands.

This means Vanessa has her hands free, and she places one on my upper arm, rubbing soothingly. "It's okay," she says. "It's gone."

Swallowing thickly, I bring my eyes to hers. "I'm sorry."

"What for?" She cocks her head, watching me intently.

"I should be able to—I need to—"

"You don't need to do anything, Sven," she says, and her usage of my name grounds me. "Misophonia is no joke."

My eyes water. "You—you know what that is?"

"Extreme sensitivity to particular sounds." She nods. "Noise sensitivity is common among autistic people, but they don't all have misophonia. Researchers are still looking for a link, though."

"How…"

Vanessa squeezes my arm. "When you first told me… I started researching. I want to help you, support you. The last thing I want is to be a burden to you or trigger you by accident. I didn't know enough about autism, and I know it's all highly relative to each person, but I needed to know the basics, and it isn't your job to educate me. That's putting more emotional labor on you, whether you want to do it or not."

I marvel at this woman. How does she just…

I love you. The words are on the tip of my lips. I want to blurt them out, I want to scream them from the rooftops.

But I don't. Because if she's not ready for marriage to be on the table, then I highly doubt she'll be okay with me definitively declaring my feelings for her, either.

Cupping her cheek with my palm, her skin feels silky soft beneath my fingertips, and her light floral perfume washes over me in a tidal wave of familiarity and comfort.

My eyes on hers, I give her every chance to pull away as I lean down and slowly brush my lips over hers. Her mouth parts on a gasp, though I'm careful to keep the kiss light and sweet, an innocent whisper of lips on lips. Her taste sends a burst of want ricocheting through me, ping-ponging off all my internal organs and coalescing deep in my gut.

Her fingers tighten on my bicep, squeezing me as tightly as a blood pressure cuff. Panic wells within me. Oh no. No, no. She doesn't like this. I need to—

I pull back.

My vision blurs, and her eyes are hazy, her lips parted as she stares up at me.

And then she sighs, relinquishing her intense hold and relaxing her grip. Vanessa moves her hand up to my shoulder, then wraps the other arm around my neck, bringing my body flush to hers.

"Hi," she whispers.

"Hi?"

I think I messed up, but her reaction doesn't seem to go along with that theory. What do I do now? How do I—

She crashes her mouth into mine, rough and needy. A wild noise escapes my throat as she licks into my mouth, her tongue tangling with mine. Tilting her head back for a better angle, I deepen the kiss. She lets out a soft pant against my mouth.

"More," she breathes.

There's a cough behind me, and slowly, I pull back. Dazed

and disoriented, I see her roommates standing on opposite sides of the room, watching us with what seems to be amusement on their faces.

"As much as I'm happy you guys like each other and everything," Elsy says, "We have a strict rule, no hooking up in the common areas of the apartment."

Vanessa glares at her roommate, even as a pretty pink blush stains her cheeks. "We weren't…"

"Girl, you were ten seconds away from climbing him like a tree," Bex cuts in. "And hey, I get it. He's hot. But Els is right. We don't need to see it happen. I'm not a voyeur, and I don't think you're really all that into exhibitionism."

My eyebrow arches up at her casual mention of kink in everyday conversation. Most people I meet in this country are far too repressed to admit to being interested in kink, much less knowledgeable about it.

Bex shrugs. "I've been re-reading some of Madison's books. I forgot how spicy he writes them."

"We're leaving now," Vanessa declares, before I can inquire who this Madison person is, and why he's writing spicy things. She removes her arms from my body, reaching down to clasp my hand. "You ready?"

"For you?" I link our fingers together and squeeze her hand. She smiles up at me. "Always."

twenty-three

. . .

Sven

THE RESTAURANT IS a quiet bistro tucked into the North End. MacGregor didn't blink when I asked for a recommendation, just gave me the name and clapped me on the shoulder.

I still don't particularly like physical touch, but when Vanessa holds my hand or leans into me, I enjoy it. When the guys slap me on the back… I mean, I deal with it. Since I know it's meant to show camaraderie, it doesn't bother me as much as when there's no reason for it.

And now… sitting across from Vanessa in the candlelight and with the soft music playing around us…

"Do you realize this is our first date?" she asks, a smile on her lips.

I jolt.

It is.

"Does that… bother you?" I venture carefully.

She cocks her head. "No, I don't think so. We went about all of this backwards. So, I guess as long as we make an effort to do this going forward, I think it'll be okay."

"It's been a long time since I went on a date," I admit quietly.

"You know all about my last relationship." She sips her wine. "When was yours?"

"It ended four years ago." Right after she started working for the team and came back into my life. "I think she's married to another hockey player now back home in Sweden. We don't keep in touch."

"Do you miss her?" It's a landmine of a question, but her expression is open and inquisitive, like she genuinely wants to know, judgment-free.

"No," I say honestly. "I haven't thought of her in years, really."

"And you haven't dated since?"

I shake my head. "It wasn't the right time."

And since Vanessa had the whole no hockey players rule…

"Why did it end?"

"I thought I was happy," I admit. "And then one day, I realized I was settling. I was fine, going through the motions, doing what I was supposed to do. Until I wasn't. So when I went home, I ended it, and she moved out two days later."

"And how long were you together?"

Pursing my lips, I try to remember. "A few years. We hadn't set a date yet, and she wasn't pushing for it, so I wasn't sure why either of us were waiting. It just… wasn't right."

Vanessa stares at me. "Set a date? Like…"

"For the wedding."

"You were engaged? And just… ended it? Like, you decided on your way to practice that she wasn't right for you, and it had to end?" She gapes at me.

"Pretty much."

I'd been walking into the training facility on a Monday morning when I smelled the scent of Vanessa's floral perfume, and the memory made me instantly rock-hard— which is not a good thing when trying to lift heavy weights in the weight room. She went on a tour of the facility an hour later, stopping in the gym, and I nearly dropped the dumbbells in my hands when I saw her.

We left that night on a road trip. When we got back on Wednesday, and I saw her in the office talking animatedly with Jacky, I just—I knew.

When I got back to the apartment, I told Marika we should talk, and then I ended it. I couldn't string her along. It wasn't fair to her to pretend when I'd found what I actually wanted. Who I actually wanted.

The fact that nothing would happen with Vanessa was irrelevant. Marika deserved better than to be someone's second choice.

"That seems… sudden."

Calm and collected, I lift my shoulders in a simple shrug, though inside I'm vibrating with anxiety. My knee bounces uncontrollably under the table.

"When you know, you really know."

"But then you didn't date. You didn't find someone else."

"Because I knew what I wanted."

Vanessa looks at me curiously over the top of her wineglass. "And what was that?"

You.

I can't say that, though.

Can I?

I don't know.

"Sven, what did you want?"

"I wanted something I couldn't have," I tell her carefully.

"And now?"

Gesturing between us with my hand, I exhale slowly. "Well, we're here now, aren't we?"

She narrows her eyes. "I don't understand."

"Your first day with the Grizzlies was Monday, September 13th," I tell her.

"What does that have to do with anything? How do you remember my hire date?"

"Because I broke things off with Marika on Wednesday, September 15th."

Vanessa stares at me.

Squaring my shoulders, I meet her eyes steadily.

"So you broke things off with your fiancée because…"

"I told you at the beginning of this, I have feelings for you."

She blinks.

"I've never hidden that. You stated quite publicly that you would not date any of the team's players. So I didn't ask you out," I tell her evenly. "That didn't change anything for me."

"But… you didn't even know me." She swallows. "You didn't say anything to me."

"We had a connection at the wedding, and I knew I wanted more. After… I needed some time to figure myself out, and then by the time I was ready, it was too late."

She cocks an eyebrow. "Figure yourself out?"

I lift a shoulder. "I didn't want you to be a rebound, and if I'd jumped straight from her to you, that's what it would have been reduced to. I think what we have—what we could have had back then—it was worth more than a fling."

Vanessa's eyes flutter a few times. "I don't know what to say."

"Is there anything to say? Can't it just be… fact?"

She sips her wine, quiet. "If I hadn't asked you to pretend, what would you have done?"

Die celibate, remembering our night together until the end of time.

"You set clear boundaries. You don't date hockey players." I swallow. "As much as I hope to have another few years to play, I would have reached out once my career ended."

"You'd wait that long? You wouldn't find someone else?"

"It wouldn't be fair to them," I shrug. "I don't ever want

to be someone's second choice, and I would never push someone to be my second choice."

"How do you know I'm the right choice?

"Because…" I take a deep breath. "I don't like physical touch. In general, I'm fairly touch averse."

Vanessa stares at me. "You play hockey."

"In hockey, they don't touch me," I explain. "There's hitting and checking, and sometimes there's fighting, but there isn't physical touch. The sensation of someone else's hand on me makes my skin crawl. Even something as innocent as a handshake can set me off."

Purposefully, I reach across the table, and I take her hand.

"I don't feel like that with you. Even with other people I've been close to, women I've dated, family members… I didn't like physical touch." I squeeze her hand. "It's not like that with you. I want the innocent physical contact when I'm with you."

"So that's why you're always putting your arm around me or holding my hand," she says quietly. She cocks her head. "Why don't you like when I put my hand on your knee?"

Swallowing, I admit: "I like that a little too much."

Her eyes go wide. "Oh."

"I'm not…" I exhale. "I'm not good with people. With explaining my thoughts. I don't think the same way other people do."

"You're doing great," she tells me. "I'm just… surprised. Processing."

"Why haven't you dated since you and Andrews…"

Vanessa pauses. "I didn't want to let anyone get close enough to hurt me again. It was easier to keep things to one night only than risk getting hurt."

The chaos of my brain goes quiet.

"He really hurt you."

She nods. "We were talking about getting married, and

then three weeks later, he dumped me. On my birthday." She shrugs. "We... well, we talked."

"Oh?"

"Last week. He told me some things that... well, I've had to reevaluate some things I've known for a long time."

My eyebrows go up.

"I can't share his secrets," she adds quickly.

"I'd never ask you to betray his confidence," I assure her. "I just want you to..."

To find closure. To find peace.

"I don't hate him anymore," Vanessa says quietly. "I carried the hurt around for a long, long time. But given what I know now... He wants to be my friend. And I don't think that's a bad idea."

"He cares deeply about you."

"I know," she says. "Does that bother you?"

"No. Because if you wanted to be with him, you would be," I tell her simply. "Instead, you asked me to pretend with you..."

Her face goes pink. "I did, yeah."

"Why me?" I've always wondered. "Was it just because I was there?"

Vanessa stares at our clasped hands for a moment. "I knew I could trust you. You wouldn't hurt me, not on purpose, and you wouldn't take advantage of me."

The thought makes me sick. "No. I would never—no."

"I know," she says quietly. She squeezes my hand. "I've always liked you, given our history, and I... I'm very glad that we're here, that we are where we are."

"Me, too," I tell her, and her smile lights up my entire world like fireworks.

We might not have started this in the traditional way, but that doesn't discount where we are. Or where we could go.

twenty-four

. . .

Vanessa

SVEN SEEMS to relax more and more the longer we sit at dinner. He finishes his glass of wine but waves off the bottle when I offer more. His eyes are bright, his face flushed, but it doesn't seem like the alcohol has gone to his head.

I think… I think it's me.

Which is absolutely ridiculous. There's no way he's serious about his supposed feelings for me. We barely know each other. He only likes the fantasy version of me he's concocted in his head.

Except… Squeezing my legs together, I ignore the ache at my core, and try to focus on what he's saying. My attention keeps getting caught on his mouth, his plush lips, the faint scruff lining his jaw, the long blond hair I want to run my fingers through…

Sven clears his throat, and I startle.

"What?" I ask.

"Are you okay?" he asks seriously. "You seem… distracted."

"I am," I admit readily.

His eyebrows go up, but he waits patiently for me to regroup.

"Do you want dessert?" he asks when I don't say anything.

I'd rather have him for dessert.

"I think we should head out," I tell him.

He blinks a few times. "Okay."

Reaching across the table, I squeeze his hand. "I think we should head out."

His eyebrows knit together. He's not getting it.

"Take me home, Sven."

His face falls. "Are you not having a good time?"

Wait.

No.

I squeeze his hand again. "I just think we'll have a better time in your bed," I say quietly.

It takes a second for him to understand. When he realizes what I'm trying to say, he swallows thickly, his grip tightening on my hand.

"Oh." He lifts his other hand, gesturing to the waiter for the check.

"Oh?" I bite the inside of my cheek, taking in his strong, broad shoulders and the sharp angle of his jaw.

"I wasn't sure if..." He clears his throat. "I would not want to pressure you."

"You aren't." If anything, I'm the one pushing him.

"Are you… ready?" His face is pained.

It's time for me to lay my cards on the table.

"I'm not in love with you," I finally say. "I don't know if I ever will be. I want to be, but that's not the same thing. I don't have feelings for anyone else, and I'm not interested in pursuing anyone else. I want you."

The naked desire in his eyes makes me want to crawl under the table and hide away. Still, I persevere.

"I want to be in a healthy place where I can feel my feelings and be confident in them," I tell him. "I'm not there yet.

I'm working on getting there. After all these years… I have closure."

He presses his lips together. "Andrews."

"And me."

I believed I was unlovable. That's why Robby left me when we were talking about forever.

I believed I was unworthy of love. That was why my parents split up and started new families without me.

I believed I was incapable of love. That's why I stuck to one-night stands and quick flings rather than expose my heart.

"I'm starting to come around to the idea that maybe I was wrong about some core fundamental thoughts." Okay, a lot of them. "It's going to take some time to rewire my brain and think differently."

Taking a breath, I meet his gaze steadily.

"But I'm willing to put in the work. It's worth doing—for you, for us."

His breath catches. "Vanessa—"

"Take me home, Sven," I tell him. "Take me to your bed and love me, so that I can learn to love you, too."

He gets out of his chair and walks around to my side, ducking down. He cups my cheek in his hand and kisses me sweetly.

"As you wish," he murmurs, pulling away.

Briskly, he walks across the restaurant, and I see him speak in hushed tones with the waiter before he pulls out his wallet. Handing the waiter several bills, Sven turns on his heel and strides toward me. He cuts an impressive figure as he glides through the restaurant as easily as if he were on skates.

Tonight, he's wearing a dark blue three-piece suit with a yellow tie that's nearly gold, or maybe that's just the golden flecks in his green eyes. His long hair is loose to his shoulders, giving real-life Viking vibes. *There's a reason I read so much historical Viking romance…*

And he's mine.

He offers his hand and I take it, rising immediately from my seat. When I reach for my coat, it's to find he's holding it, ready to help me. When my arms are in the sleeves, he pulls the coat over my shoulders and around to my front, using the lapels to tug me forward.

Leaning down, he brushes his lips across mine, the barest whisper of a kiss that leaves me wanting more.

The valet brings the car around and Sven helps me in before jogging around to the driver's side. After he shifts the car into gear, he takes my hand again, lacing our fingers together over the console.

His Beacon Hill townhouse looks the same, quiet and unassuming with flower baskets beneath the windows. Even in the cool winter weather, the plants are thriving. Inside, the stark contrast of the black floors and white walls with the greenery make the place feel so much more welcoming than they did the last time I was here.

"Where's Rupert?" I ask as Sven takes my coat, hanging it in the closet beside his.

He nods toward a giant birdcage in the corner, with a sheet drawn over it. "She goes to sleep around sundown. Don't worry, she'll be awake early in the morning."

"I can't wait to meet her. Properly," I add. "I don't know that I made the best impression last time."

"She'll love you," he says, and my breath catches. "Because I already do."

"Sven…"

He shakes his head. "I know you have work to do. That's fine. I've been dancing around my feelings for you for some time. I didn't want to scare you off further."

"Because the marriage talk after our first kiss wasn't enough?" I try for a teasing smile.

His eyes are warm like molten honey as he shrugs. "I'm

not good at reading between the lines. I don't see the gray area," he says. "I do best when things are explicitly spelled out, and you deserve the same."

Sven takes my hand. "I love you, and when you're ready, I want to build a life with you. I want us to have a future together. However long it takes to get there, I can wait. I'll be here—for you."

I bite my lip. "How do you know you won't change your mind again?"

"I won't."

"But how do you know?" My heart hammers in my chest, wanting desperately to believe him.

"Because you are all I've ever wanted, even when it wasn't an option," he says. "Why would I throw away the very thing I've been dreaming about since we met nine years ago?"

I lose my breath.

"It—nine years ago? That long?"

He nods. "From the very first night we met."

If I had any lingering doubts, they've fizzled away.

I hold out my hand and Sven takes it, lacing our fingers together.

"Take me to your bed," I tell him. "Let me love you the way I know how."

He pulls me close for a soft, sweet kiss.

I don't want soft.

I don't want sweet.

twenty-five

. . .

Vanessa

MY FINGERS DIG into his scalp, twisting his wavy hair. Beneath the longer strands, the sides are shaved, and the sharp texture change sends prickles of pleasure to my core.

Sven breaks the kiss. Before I can so much as blink, he scoops me up over his shoulder. His hand on my ass, he starts up the stairs.

Letting out a laugh, I smack his ass, and I'm rewarded by a soft pant rumbling from his mouth.

The last time I was here, I didn't get to see his room. Now, upside down, I like what I can see. It's the same dark flooring and light walls, and in the darkness, I can make out some plants without much detail. He slaps on a lamp and the room floods with warm, golden light.

Sven deposits me on the edge of the bed. Before I can so much as blink, he's on his knees before me, staring up at me with heat in his green eyes.

I cup his cheek, and he leans into the contact, brushing his stubbly jaw against my skin as he turns to place a kiss in the center of my palm.

"The last time we were together…" His voice is hoarse. He clears his throat. "You took care of me. You made me feel seen. Wanted. I'd never experienced that before, and since then…"

I don't want to hear about whatever's happened since then. I don't want to know about the other women who came before me.

"Everything I've wanted centered around this, around us," he says. "I've been searching for nine years, trying to recreate that same feeling."

I swallow. "And? How is this measuring up to your fantasy?"

"It's pretty great," he says, his eyes on mine.

"Oh? Only pretty great?"

"Well, it could be better."

He traces a figure eight on the inside of my knee. The feel of his warm skin on mine, even separated by the thin layer of my tights, sends lightning bolts of lust through me.

Chemistry is a powerful drug. I've wanted plenty of guys before. I've been interested.

But I've never had someone gazing back at me like he does, molten honey and desire clearly etched across his features.

I raise my eyebrows. "How could it be better?"

"Well, I'd quite like to bury my face in your cunt," he says.

A sharp bolt of lust ricochets through me. The sweet, polite contrast of his request and his naughty words are as enticing as he is.

"Is that acceptable to you?" he asks.

I'm unable to do much more than nod, and his half-smirk turns into a full, genuine smile.

Sven sits back on his heels, and to my surprise, he takes my ankle in his hands. With deft, delicate fingers, he unbuckles the thin straps of my heel, pulling the shoe away and running his thumb up the arch of my foot before he turns his attention to the other shoe, doing the same.

My hands shift under my dress, reaching for the waistband of my tights.

Rising above me, Sven scoops me up again and places me at the center of the bed, so my head rests on his pillows. He catches my hand and covers it with his.

Together, we pull down my tights, and as he peels them off my legs, a heady dose of want courses through me. His thumb trails over my center, over my panties. My hips tilt up and a soft whimper bursts from my lips. I need more.

"You're good?" He checks in, his eyes rising to mine.

Nodding eagerly, I try to spread my legs for him.

But he shakes his head.

Our first time together, I definitely took the lead, so I'm not expecting him to flip me around onto my hands and knees. I arch back against him.

His fingertips sketch the column of my spine, the skin exposed by the dress erupting into goosebumps. My hair tumbles over my shoulder as I look back at him.

"Like what you see?"

His eyes are dark when they meet mine.

"Yes," he states definitively. His eyes flutter shut and he tightens his hands on my hips. "Yes."

"I'm yours," I tell him.

Hiking up the bottom of my dress over my ass, Sven peels my panties down—but only a little bit. The elastic constricting my thighs means I can't spread my legs as far as I'd like.

Cool air hits my exposed pussy. It does nothing to cool me down.

I look over my shoulder again. He's staring at me, want plain on his face. His thumb brushes over my center, trailing through the wetness. It's not enough. I need more.

My heart hammers in my chest. This is more than just sex to him. He has feelings for me, real feelings, and has for some time. How do we do this?

The first press of his hot, wet tongue to my core makes me yelp. Sven tightens his hands on my hips and tilts his head, applying more pressure right below my clit. Unabashed, I push my hips back into his face.

His groan vibrates through me. He shifts, spreading me, opening me up for him. Before I can think too much about how utterly exposed I feel, Sven dives back in, licking at me with strong, steady pressure.

The soft prickle of his facial hair sparks little lightning bolts of sensation between my legs.

The grip of his fingers around my thigh just might leave faint bruises tomorrow.

And the noises he makes are obscene. And so fucking sexy.

As his fingers trace my seam, I push my hips back again, asking for more. He slips one finger inside of me, slow and steady.

It's good. I like it.

But I need more.

And as he adds a second finger, twisting and scissoring, I know that I can trust him to give me what I want. What I need.

His tongue laves over my clit, sucking at me with far more finesse than he had nine years ago. The thick press of his fingers pumping inside of me has me clenching around him. Everything inside of me stretches tight and taut. I'm a shard of glass about to shatter.

But I trust him. He'll put me back together.

As I start to splinter, his hand on my hip keeps me tethered to this plane of existence. The pleasure bursts within me, my entire being imploding in the best way possible. I come with a cry.

But Sven is there. He doesn't stop. His fingers keep the same rhythm, his mouth keeps the same pressure, giving me exactly what I need.

It's too much. My arms give out and I start to collapse to the bed.

He slides his arm around to my shoulder, steadying me. I take the support he gives so effortlessly. He pulls his fingers out of me, and before I can think about how empty I feel, he lays me out on the bed, letting me crash onto the pillows.

He collapses beside me. His hand settles on my lower back, just above the top of my dress.

Pillowing my head on my arms, I turn to face him. He's wearing a pleased expression, his beard glistening from… me.

I swallow. Emotions I can't identify bubble up within me. I'm not ready for them.

I don't—

I can't—

Sven rubs my lower back. The heavy weight of his warm palm on my skin keeps the emotions at bay. His green eyes are kind as he takes me in, no doubt cataloging my messy hair and the bags under my eyes and makeup smeared across my face.

He's looking at me like I'm the most beautiful person he's ever seen. And for the first time, I feel like it might actually be possible.

Before I can second-guess myself, I launch myself at him, burrowing into his side. My arm slings over his belly, my leg over his as I cling to him. Tears come to my eyes. I blink a few times to hide my reaction. Some of the wetness seeps out of the corner of my eyes, and I press my face deeper into his chest. His scent surrounds me, spicy and fresh with a hint of musk.

He holds me.

He holds me, and he lets me feel my feelings, and he doesn't try to push me along. He's so patient with me—in this, in everything he does.

I come back to myself slowly.

I'm aware of the scratchy material of his waistcoat beneath

my cheek. The buttons are pressed along the ridge of my nose, and that's not very comfortable. My dress is twisted all around me, my panties pulled down along my thighs, and I'm wet—very wet.

But it's his hand on my exposed back, roving up and down my spine with a careful caress. It's the expansion of his chest beneath my cheek with every breath he takes. It's the solid planes of his body wrapped around mine, my leg between his, my arm over his belly.

It's the physical sensations that I recognize first.

I almost don't realize how safe I feel. How comfortable. This man brought me to tears with the tender, thorough way he loved me.

Loves me.

And for the first time... I start to think that maybe, I can love him, too.

twenty-six

. . .

Sven

VANESSA'S BREATH slows to a moderate pace. She's not panting like she's just run a marathon—or had a fantastic orgasm—and she's not choked up like she might cry again.

When I peek down at her face, she's calm and relaxed. Pliant.

Her hand moves from my belly up to my sternum, and she looks up at me, a satisfied smile on her face. Her blonde waves are messy, and her makeup is smeared over her face—and she's absolutely the most gorgeous woman I've ever seen.

How the hell did we get here? How did I get so lucky as to get this second chance with her?

One thing's for certain: I'm not going to waste this opportunity with her. I waited for her for nine years. I can wait a little longer for her to be ready.

Vanessa arches up against me as she moves her legs to remove her panties, shuffling up the bed until she can set her hand on my cheek, and she lowers my head down for a kiss. She lets out a groan, no doubt tasting herself on my lips. Deepening the kiss, she slips her tongue into my mouth, tangling with my own.

As I slide my arm more firmly around her, I shift us so we're both on our side, facing each other. I draw her leg up over my hip, opening her up again—but I don't touch her.

She tries to pull me on top of her, tries to rub her core against me. The sensation of her hot, wet cunt, brushing against me through my pants is enough to overload my brain. With everything I possess, I force myself to still.

She breaks the kiss and frowns up at me. "What's wrong?"

"Nothing's wrong."

"You're… stiff." She runs her hand down my arm. "What happened? What did I do?"

I have wanted this for so fucking long, and now that it's here… I almost don't know what to do.

This thing we have between us—it's more than just sex.

I mean, sure. She's the only person who can touch me without a full body shiver in a bad way. And she's the only person I've ever felt completely safe around. Okay, and yeah, she's the only person I've ever wanted to pursue.

It's more than that, though.

Isn't it?

I love the way she bites her lip when she's thinking, and the little furrow in her brow when she's concentrating, and the way she lets out a happy sigh after her first sip of coffee. I love the way she always has a kind word for everyone, the way she's always ready with a fist bump or high five for the guys after a good play or a goal, and the way she fits so effortlessly with the team, like she was made to be part of us.

Since the moment she walked back into my life, all of my thoughts have centered around her in one way or another. Yet I didn't even let myself consider a world in which this could ever happen.

And now that it's here…

Vanessa sets her hand on my cheek.

"Hey, it's just me," she says quietly. "This is just us."

My eyes flick to hers, so full of kindness and understanding. My throat gets choked up and I have to swallow to force all of my feelings back to a place where I can navigate them.

And that's when it hits me: this is a lot.

She told me, but I didn't understand, not really. My feelings for her aren't little, they're all-consuming... and right now they're threatening to consume me.

So how did she feel when I bombarded her with my declarations? She didn't even have the benefit of four years of wanting on her side.

"I'm sorry," I say quietly.

She tilts her head, her brow furrowed in confusion. "What for?"

"We should have dated. We should have taken this slow. I pushed you, I rushed you. That wasn't fair of me."

Vanessa runs her fingers over the short beard lining my cheek. I shiver—in a good way.

"However we got here, I'm glad that we did," she says. "We're going into this with our eyes wide open and our feet firmly planted. We're making healthy, mature decisions." She trails her thumb over my bottom lip. "And that is what will make this work."

"I hope it does."

She takes the opportunity to press her thumb past the crease of my lips, and automatically I suck and swirl my tongue around her finger.

A heady dose of want courses through me. I'm powerless against her; she holds all the cards. I'd do anything she asks.

Vanessa removes her thumb, running the wet digit down my chin and to the hollow of my throat. Her fingers rest lightly around my neck, exerting the tiniest bit of pressure.

I swallow.

She smiles.

Surging forward, I meet her halfway for a kiss. It's rough, needy. Her tongue flicks into my mouth and her fingers tighten on my neck. She's not constricting my airway, just letting me know she's there.

She's in control.

She's in charge.

And I like that.

My cock jerks in my pants, and I know she feels it, pressed up against me as she is, because she smiles against my mouth. I pull her leg over my hip, grinding into her to relieve some of the pressure.

Her bare, wet cunt is hot and slick, and even with my suit pants in the way, it feels absolutely amazing. I don't know if I can wait to be inside her again.

Vanessa removes her hand from around my throat. I can't stop the disappointed whine that bursts out.

But then—

She moves her hands to my waistcoat, unbuttoning it quickly, and I disconnect from her to pull it off. Her nimble fingers work quickly at my shirt, focusing on the buttons there.

With three freed, she groans and tears at the middle of the shirt, ripping the fabric and sending buttons flying.

Helping her, I remove the shirt, tossing it on the floor behind us. Her hands go to work on my belt, whipping the leather free. The whistle of the leather through the straps makes me shiver.

Vanessa pauses. "Are you okay?"

"No, I'm not," I tell her honestly.

"Is it a bad sound?"

Shaking my head, I pop the button and zip on my pants. "It's a very good sound."

"Then…"

Taking her hand in mine, I guide her into my open pants, and she grips my shaft automatically. I tighten her fist around me to get the pressure I need.

"This. This is what you do to me."

She strokes my cock slowly, tortuously slowly. I think I might die. I honestly think I could come just from this. I might want to.

If this is how I go… yeah, I'm okay with that.

She's still wearing her dress, though. That's not okay. That's not right.

Pulling her hand away, I scoot back. She's watching me intently. I can't read the expression on her face.

There's a zipper on the side of her dress. As I pull down the tab and cleave away the fabric, she sighs and helps me. It's a pretty dress. I like it on her. But I like it even better on my floor.

When I finally have her bare to me, I reach for her again.

But Vanessa shakes her head. "We need to have a conversation."

"Now?" I set my hand on her hip. "What do we need to talk about?"

"I'm on birth control," she says.

"Okay. And?"

"And I know the team tests you regularly. I've been tested since—well, I'm good," she says. "But I'm not ready for kids, I want us to be in a different place if that happens." Her eyes meet mine. "Not if. *When.*"

Swallowing thickly, I nod. "Okay." She's meeting me halfway. She's not saying she doesn't want it. She's just not ready for it right now.

"I just—I'd feel better if we used condoms, too," Vanessa whispers. Her shoulders go up around her ears. "Is that okay?"

I blink. "Why wouldn't that be okay?"

She swallows. "I know some guys don't like them, and, well…"

"I'm not *some guy*, I'm yours," I tell her. "And my first priority is always going to be making you feel safe and comfortable and loved. Always. What you're asking isn't unreasonable. So yes—until you're ready to go without, there's no reason not to use condoms. Contraception is both of our responsibilities, but you'd have the burden to bear. You're already taking a medication that has a profound impact on you. Using condoms is hardly asking me for the same sort of commitment."

Vanessa blinks a few times. "You're just... you..." She shakes her head. "Who are you?"

Rolling away, I offer her my hand. "Hi, I'm Sven. I'm your boyfriend."

twenty-seven

. . .

Sven

SHE STARES at me for a few minutes. Blinks.

And then she bursts into peals of laughter.

And I smile, because I did that. I made her laugh.

Vanessa shakes my hand, then pulls me into her, until she's wrapped up in my arms again. Holding on tightly, I breathe in her light floral perfume and close my eyes. This is —I could do this forever.

"I really like you."

My breath catches. It still doesn't feel real.

And when her hand slips off my chest to trail down my stomach, I almost stop her. This is perfect as it is.

But when she wraps her hand around my cock and gives me a slow, firm stroke? Yeah, I like this, too.

Her lips meet mine on a sigh, and as she winds her free arm around my neck, I cup my hand over hers and tighten her grip around my throat.

Vanessa's eyes fly open. "You like this?"

She flexes her fingers.

My cock jerks in her fist.

She smiles.

"I guess you do."

Crushing my mouth against hers, I try to wordlessly show her exactly how much I do like this. My hands travel up her sides to her breasts, covering the firm flesh, my fingers stroking the underside of her breast in a feather-light touch.

She inhales sharply.

So I do it again.

Her nipples are firm, tight pebbles against my palm and I grind down with pressure, massaging the swell of her breasts. My thumb slips down and I tug.

Vanessa's hand tightens on my throat. She's not choking me—I can still breathe—but the slight constriction is heady and powerful.

I nudge her hand away from my cock. She lets out a disappointed noise, sliding her hand lower, cupping my balls. Her hand is sticky with pre-cum. The sensation of her slick fingers wrapping around my balls makes my eyes flutter shut.

She tugs.

My cock jerks against her wrist.

She slides two fingers beneath my sack, to rub against my perineum.

I bolt upright as a wave of heat threatens to overtake me. I had no idea I was so sensitive right there — it's a completely different kind of toe-curling stimulation when she does it than when I touch myself there.

And as Vanessa smirks up at me, I have a feeling she knows exactly what she's doing.

While I'm up, I squirm away, and she immediately releases me. I wiggle my way across the bed to the nightstand and from the drawer I pull a box of condoms and some lube.

Vanessa peers at the box curiously.

"What?"

"It's not opened." She looks at me. "How long have you had them?"

"About twelve hours." I glance at the clock. "Okay, closer to fifteen. I picked them up this morning."

She smirks. "Oh? Thought you were getting lucky tonight?"

With a shrug, I tear open the box and rip off a foil square, tossing the rest of the box back into the nightstand. "I was hoping."

Her face splits into a wide smile. "Me, too."

I pause. It takes me a second to figure out if she's making fun of me. But the longer I watch her face, the more I'm able to recognize the genuine happiness in her voice.

Vanessa takes the condom from my hand, ripping it open. She puts the latex circle on the head of my dick, and as she rolls it down my shaft, her grip is tight and firm, the pressure excruciatingly perfect. She reaches for the lube and this time I take it away from her. Slicking my fingers, I reach for the apex of her thighs and slide two fingers inside of her.

Her eyes flutter shut. She's slick and wet, but a little extra lube is never a bad thing.

I keep a quick, powerful pace, circling my thumb against her clit. She gasps and arches against me, pushing her pelvis into me. I bring her to the edge.

And then as she goes tense and her walls start to flutter, I stop.

Vanessa opens her eyes to glare at me. "Excuse me. What are you doing?"

"Oh? Did you want to come?" My smile teases my lips.

She arches her back, thrusting against my fingers. "Yes."

"Oh, okay then." I slide my fingers from within her. Even though I already know she tastes incredible, I can't resist the urge to lick my fingers clean.

"Sven." She huffs out a breath. "You're being mean."

Rolling onto my back, I pull her with me until she's sprawled on top of me, her smaller body a pleasant weight on top of mine. Almost like my weighted blanket. Except better, because we're both naked, and she smells and tastes amazing, and...

Vanessa rises up onto her knees. She grasps my cock and puts the tip at her entrance. My hands move immediately to her hips.

I expect her to go slow. I expect her to tease, to take her time.

What I'm not expecting? Her to slide down onto me, the slick glide of her cunt around me so fucking perfect I lose my breath and all ability to think.

She fucks herself on my cock until I'm as deep as I can go. Planting her hands on my chest, her nails curling into my pecs, Vanessa lifts up and sinks back down. My eyes roll back into my head. She rolls her hips, grinding her clit against my pelvis.

As I move my thumb to rub her clit, she inhales sharply and then clenches around me. I urge her up, thrust up into her. She grunts. Her nails dig into my pecs in a sharp-sweet bite.

Urging her down, I splay my hand on her back, and she folds down until her chest is pressed to mine.

When her skin touches mine, it's like every nerve ending lights on fire—in the best possible way. I feel safe and seen, like she can see inside my soul and see the truth of who I am. There's an incredible intimacy in knowing the way someone moves and tastes and feels. It's not awkward in the slightest as we try new angles and rhythms. It's… comfortable.

This is what I've been looking for and never been able to recreate.

And reality? It's so much better than my memory of the last time we were together.

A part of me worried I was too caught up in the fantasy for this to work. I didn't want to hyperfixate on a memory that was faulty from the beginning.

But this—we're good at this. It's like there's a lock inside my chest, and she's the key that clicks into place.

I don't need her. I can survive without her. I'm a whole and complete person even without a partner.

But I don't want to do this without her.

And as I thrust up into her and my hands trace her smooth skin, I know that this is it for me. This is what I've been searching for. My body buzzes with overstimulation and it's difficult to focus on any one thing.

Vanessa kisses me, her mouth hot and needy, and I return my attention to us and what we're doing. She feels amazing, her greedy cunt welcoming me eagerly. Her hand is on my throat, not exerting pressure, just resting there, letting me know she could if she wanted.

And I think I want her to.

Working my hand between us, I touch her where we're joined. Her breath catches. I urge her upright again, then lean forward to fuse my mouth to her tit, laving on the pebbled nipple with my tongue. I bite gently on the sensitive bud and suck away the sting.

She comes with a cry, her fingers spasming around my throat, and that's all I need to let go. Her slick channel clenches around me. My thrusts become erratic as I chase that high. Pleasure shoots up my spine and I erupt, releasing into the condom.

Vanessa slumps against me, her arms loose around my neck. Rolling her onto her back, I deal with the condom and then pull her into my arms. Her head pillows on my pec, her fingers tracing the divots of my abs.

"I forgot," she says, breathing hard.

"What did you forget?" I catch her hand with mine, bringing her knuckles to my lips, then tuck her palm against my chest.

"How good this can be with the right person." She swallows, looking up at me. "With my forever person."

twenty-eight

. . .

Vanessa

I CAN'T WIPE the smile off my face. All week long at work, people give me knowing smirks. I'm sure they can guess what goes on between me and Sven after hours. For each of the four-game home stretch, between games, I stay at Sven's place. In the evenings, I go to the game, watching from the pit. During the break between periods, he's focused on the game, but as soon as the final buzzer sounds, he wraps me up in a hug in front of everyone.

I'm on my lunch break when he enters the lounge, whistling as he pours himself a coffee and adds about an inch of creamer.

Wait.

He doesn't drink coffee creamer.

As I watch, he pulls down a second mug and adds a small splash of almond milk to it, then joins me across the room.

"Hey," he says, setting the first mug in front of me. "How's your day going?"

"Not bad."

Waking up in his arms was heaven. It was everything I wanted and didn't know I needed. There's a calmness in my soul. I hadn't realized it was so disruptive, so jittery. Now that everything is still… it's like I can breathe again.

"Do you want to grab dinner tonight?" Sven asks.

"Pick me up at seven?" I have to run home and get a few things ready. Tomorrow, we hit the road again with a trip to D.C. and then Buffalo.

He grins at me, squeezing my hand.

We sit in easy silence as the players and staff filter in and out of the lounge. A few people give us a smile or a nod, but most leave us alone. They're getting used to seeing us together.

Robby waltzes into the lounge and makes a protein shake. He grins when he sees me, ambling over to us.

"Hey, Nessie," he says quietly. "You doing okay?"

I nod. "I am, yeah."

"Good." He gives me a soft smile, then turns to Sven. "You treating our girl right?"

To my surprise, Sven doesn't get upset at his calling me their girl.

"Always," he says. He looks up at Robby. "Do you want to sit?"

My ex looks surprised, then pleased. "Yeah. Thanks."

I've spent so much time ignoring him, I haven't noticed if he's made friends yet. Does he have people here? I have Jacky and Patrice, I guess even Scott is okay, but does he have anyone? What about in the city at large? He's been on the road for so long. It's hard, isolating, especially when you have to start over all the time.

"Do you have any plans for the holidays? Going home?" Sven asks Robby.

"Nah. My parents and I don't talk anymore," he says easily.

My eyebrows go up. "You don't?" His enmeshment with his family was a big bone of contention in the two and a half years we were together.

"They didn't like the last person I dated and made clear I wasn't part of the family any longer," Robby says with a lightness to his tone. "It's better this way."

I set my hand on his arm, squeezing gently, and he gives me a sad smile.

"How about you guys? Meeting the parents?"

Sven shakes his head. "My parents are in Sweden. They don't visit." His words are crisp and cool, trying to be unaffected, but his eyes are sad. The estrangement must weigh on him more than I thought.

"Nessie?"

"I got a holiday email card from my mother."

Robby's eyebrows raise. "That good?"

My shoulder lifts in a halfhearted shrug. "Her kids are cute. I think the oldest one is in high school, maybe college."

"You still don't talk to them?"

"Not since graduation." That was the last time I invited both of my parents anywhere—and neither of them wanted to take off for two days to come see me walk across that stage for my diploma.

Sven threads our fingers together, lending support.

"It's better this way. I have Elsy and Bex and Wyatt, and now I have Sven, and…"

"People always ask why I have no relationship with my parents," Robby says. "It's complicated."

"We'll make our own family," Sven says.

Robby looks between us, his eyes dropping to my belly. "Are you—you're not p—"

"No. No." I shake my head quickly.

"Family is what you make it," Sven continues. "We can pick and choose the people we keep in our lives. The people who mean the most to us. Biology doesn't make a family." He squeezes my hand. "Love does."

Robby swallows thickly. "I'm glad you two have each other."

"Now we just have to find you your happily ever after," I tell him lightly.

But he shakes his head. "Nah. I don't think that's in the cards for me."

"Come on. You can—"

"Not without making some personal sacrifices I'm not ready to make," he says quietly, firmly.

With a sigh, I relent. "Okay. I can see that." He doesn't have to come out publicly until he's ready. With his role as assistant equipment manager on the ice every game, he leads a semi-public life, and the fans are viciously intent on learning every single thing about the team and the staff.

"I just started figuring out my life without playing hockey," Robby says. "I'm still working out the rest of it. I'll get there."

Sven looks at me, then my hand on Robby's arm, and I hastily move it away. "Well, you'll always have a place in our family," he announces.

My eyes go wide. "What do you mean?"

"He cares about you, and you care about him," he says, meeting my gaze steadily. "We all have shitty enough families that we deserve the chance to start over and build something new. So, if you're okay with it…"

"I am. But you know he and I—" Waving my hand between my ex and me, I lose my nerve. "We used to… we were…"

Robby chokes.

Sven looks at him for the briefest moment, then back to me.

"Do you plan on sleeping with him?" he asks, genuine curiosity in his voice. "Do you want to be with him?"

"No! Not at all. We've talked about this. You and I—we're committed. That's… it's entirely different."

Robby is my past. The history. Sven is my future.

And to my surprise, that doesn't scare me nearly as much as it used to.

Sven squeezes my hand. "Then whatever happened between you, it's in the past. All we can do is move forward. And frankly, we could all use a little more love in our lives."

twenty-nine

. . .

Sven

BRAD CALLS me at the indecent hour of eight o'clock in the morning again. I have half a mind to decline the call. I don't want anything to ruin the heaven of Vanessa in my bed.

With lead in my stomach, I answer. There are only two reasons he's calling me: the Grizzlies want to trade me, or I've fucked up once again.

"What the fuck did you do, bud?" Brad snaps.

Fishing my sweats off the floor, I step into them and tiptoe across the room so I don't wake Vanessa. She murmurs in her sleep, but doesn't wake.

"What do you mean?"

"Management called me to discuss your contract," he snaps.

Lead sits heavy in my belly. "They want to get rid of me?"

Brad snorts. "Fuck no. They want to extend you."

I slip on the stairs. "What?"

"They low-balled you. I think we can get more—"

"Whatever they want, I'll take it," I tell him.

"What? Fuck that. We'll counter."

"I want to stay in Boston," I say firmly. "Whatever money or term they offer—I want it."

"We can always negotiate," Brad pushes.

"Is there a good term?"

"Five years, no trade."

Closing my eyes, I let out a shaky exhale. "Take it. I want it."

"Bud, this could be your last big contract. You don't want to push for seven?"

"I'm good with five more years. The no trade clause is more important."

"You'd be worth so much more on the open market," he warns.

"This is what I want. I want to stay. Hell, I'd do it for the league minimum salary."

I can hear his wince. "You can't say shit like that."

"Why? Because it's true?"

He sighs. "Because one day, someone is going to take you at your word."

"But I mean it. I would."

Hockey is incredibly important to me. It's all I ever wanted, everything I wanted to do since I was so young, when I didn't even know the difference between dreams and reality.

Dreams change. People evolve. What I wanted five years ago is not what I am searching for now.

I'm not searching anymore. I've found her.

There's a creak on the stairs and I turn to see a sleepy Vanessa making her way down. She's wearing one of my t-shirts and a pair of fuzzy socks, her legs bare. Her blonde hair is an adorable mess.

"Good morning," I say, turning on the coffee pot. If we're up, might as well take advantage of it. "Did I wake you?"

She shakes her head. "I woke up and you were gone."

Crossing the room, she makes her way to where I'm stand-ing, immediately folding her arms around my waist and snuggling into me.

"I'll be here. I'll always be here."

She gives me a sleepy smile. "Okay." She brushes her lips against mine in a brief kiss. "What did Brad want?"

"How did you know it was Brad?"

Vanessa cracks a grin. "Who else calls at this indecent hour?"

Smoothing my hand over her hair, I hold her close. "They want to extend me."

Immediately, she pulls back to look at me. "They do?"

I nod.

"Of course they do! You're awesome!" She squeezes me around the middle. "Oh, I'm so happy for you!"

"They still have to work out some details and I have to go into the office to sign the paperwork, but looks like I'll be sticking around for at least five more years." I swallow. "After that..."

"After that, we'll take it as it comes," she says. "Together."

"You're still in this with me?"

She nods. "You and me—we're the future. We're going to do this. That doesn't mean I'm unsure about my feelings. It just means one step at a time."

With a lump in my throat, I nod. "And you'll tell me if anything changes?"

Vanessa cups my cheek with her palm. "Absolutely."

There's a caw from the other room, and I sigh. "Rupert's awake."

"She's going to be so upset with you," she chides. "You didn't immediately tell her."

"Rupert's a bird," I remind her.

"Don't tell her that," Vanessa laughs. "C'mon, let's go get her."

She's only been at my place for a few wake-ups, but already she knows the routine, taking off Rupert's cover and opening the bird's cage. To my surprise, Rupert immediately flocks to her instead of to me.

"Hey, big girl," Vanessa says, stroking her feathers. "How was your night?"

"Good girl," Rupert caws. She nuzzles into Vanessa. "Rupert, good girl."

I think I finally understand what people mean when they say their heart gets ten times bigger. There's a warmth in my chest, a fuzzy pressure that takes my breath away and makes my heart beat faster.

Vanessa and Rupert are the two most important parts of my life, outside of hockey, and now… now I get to have all three. It's something I couldn't fathom even a few weeks ago, much less four years ago when I first saw her again.

Rupert launches off of Vanessa's arm and comes to stand on my shoulder. She butts her head against mine. "Good girl," my parrot says.

Vanessa comes to stand beside me, tucking her head under my chin. I hug her close.

This is what people mean when they say they've found their home. If I absolutely had to, I'd give up hockey if it meant I could spend the rest of my life with them.

I've found my home.

thirty

• • •

Vanessa

ON THE THIRD Thursday of every month, we have book club. It's the highlight of my month.

The dusty bookstore is warm and filled with laughter and good cheer. When I show up with a bottle of bourbon and a tray of holiday cookies Jacky foisted on me as I left the office, a raucous cheer goes through the assembled crowd.

I stop in and say hi to Ceci, who's wearing a floor-length crimson velvet dress and chandelier earrings — I'm not entirely sure *why* she's so dressed up, just that it doesn't surprise me. Arielle has brought Asher, Johanna came with Sullivan. I make a mental note to introduce them to Sven. I think the six of us could have a fun time.

Bex and Elsy are chatting with Rachel. Madison is lounging in the recliner with his eyes closed, enjoying a rare night off from parenting his five younger siblings. Nikki and Sofia are pouring drinks as people come in. Kiley, the youngest of our group at nineteen, runs in looking like her hair is on fire.

"What's wrong?" three or four people immediately ask her.

"Gotta pee!" She darts toward the back room.

Shaking my head, I check my watch again. Sven has a team dinner—Scott is coordinating, giving me the night off.

The bell over the door chimes.

Robby steps through the door, brushing the light snow off his dark hair. He cuts an impressive figure in his dark gray coat, with his wide shoulders and broad stature.

"You made it!" I smile as he heads toward me.

"Thanks for inviting me," he says, bumping my shoulder with his.

Bex breaks off her conversation, making her way over to us.

"Hey, Robby," she says evenly. "It's been a while."

"Yeah. It has," he says quietly. "It's good to see you again."

"You two are good?" She looks between us.

Robby nods. "I'm guessing you know," he says awkwardly. "About me."

Bex bites her lip. "Yeah."

"I didn't mean to out you. I didn't think you would hang out again," I admit.

To my surprise, Robby smiles. "I'm not out at work. I don't care if my friends know." He meets her eyes. "And I hope I can count you a friend again, Bex."

She swallows. "Yeah. You can."

"Come on, let's mingle," I tell them. "We can introduce you to some people."

The place is packed. People are still shopping for holiday presents. There's a constant onslaught of the door chiming every time it opens.

But when the place empties out and Sadie flips the closed sign on the door, it's just the core book club in the back of the shop.

Arielle raises her eyebrows at me. "And who is this?"

"This is Robby," I introduce him to the group.

Johanna frowns. "I thought you were dating Sven."

"I am. Robby's my ex." I blow out a breath. "We're working on being friends again. He just moved to town."

"Hey, dude," Sullivan says, nodding across the circle at him. "Nice to meet you. I'm Sully, this is Asher. We'll introduce you to some people around here."

Lying back in the recliner, Madison cracks open his eyes and studies him carefully. "Yeah, you can hang."

Robby exhales a heavy breath. "Thanks. I'd like that."

Ceci grins. "I thought you don't like second chances?"

Robby winks at me.

"Turns out… sometimes, we all need a second chance. I messed things up with Sven, but he still gave me another shot."

"Hell," Bex says, "The two of you getting together in the first place is already your second chance."

Nodding, I accept that. "So the least I can do is offer Robby a fresh start. As friends," I'm quick to add, when Madison opens his mouth. "This is not a poly / menage / why choose situation."

He raises an eyebrow. "I wasn't going to presume."

Sadie laughs. "Yeah, you were."

Madison sighs. "Okay, so maybe I was already envisioning this epic scene where—you know what? I'll just write it instead."

She pats his arm. "Okay, babe. Sounds good."

We go around the circle with introductions. Several people have brought their partner with them for our holiday party. It's nice to meet these people we've heard so much about from our friends.

There's a knock on the door.

"We're closed," half a dozen people call out.

The person is undeterred, knocking again.

"It's Elijah," Asher says with a broad grin, and Sadie rolls her eyes at her best friend's fiancé and his joke about Passover.

"Wrong holiday." She musses his curls as she moves toward the door. "Oh, hello there."

"I'm here with Vanessa," a crisp Swedish accent says.

My stomach flutters. It's Sven.

What's he doing here?

There's a click as the door locks again, and then Sadie appears with my boyfriend behind her, holding two loaves of sourdough bread he made this morning.

"You're not at the dinner?"

Tonight we were supposed to stay apart, each at our own place for the first time in a week. I haven't spent nearly enough time with my roommates lately. I've missed them.

As I'm half-rising out of my seat, he cuts through the circle and kisses me softly, a simple peck, before he takes my hand and sits in the empty chair beside my own.

Without me noticing, everyone moved over so we could sit together.

"I wanted to see you. Meet your friends."

A few of them sigh.

"Guys, this is Sven," I introduce, waving at the group. "These are my friends."

He nods at the crowd of people, their eyes focused on him. "Hello. I brought bread."

"Excellent," Johanna says. "We love a good carb."

"Tell us about yourself," Ceci cuts in. She leans forward, her dark eyes bright.

"Well, I play hockey."

Madison raises an eyebrow. "A sports romance?"

"Workplace and forced proximity," Sadie adds. "What else?"

"Um…" I bite my lip.

"Second chance," Bex chimes in.

Ceci grins at me. "Second chance isn't so bad after all, is it?"

I have to shake my head. "Okay, fine. It's not the worst trope in the world."

Robby turns to look at me. "You know, I don't think I ever did hear the story of how you two got together."

My face goes red. "That's because… well…"

"We met nine years ago," Sven says. "I didn't see her again until four years ago, and as soon as we met, I knew."

"You've been together for four years?" Robby looks between us. "That's a long time to keep things from the team."

"No, uh…" I swallow. Why am I so nervous? It's not like I have any reason to be embarrassed here. "We've been dating since your first day."

He frowns. "Huh?"

"We were pretend dating. Fake dating," I elaborate awkwardly.

"It wasn't fake for me," Sven says quietly, and I squeeze his hand.

"Right. I refused to date any hockey players, especially the ones on my team. But then… well, you were there, and I didn't know what to do, so…" I take a breath. "I asked Sven to be my fake boyfriend because I didn't want you to think… I don't know. It was ridiculous."

Robby looks between us. "So, let me get this straight: you decided that seeing me again was so awful, the easiest thing was to pretend to date someone else?"

I pause. "Yes."

He howls with laughter, slapping his knee. "Oh, Nessie, I love you." He squeezes my shoulder. "I'm totally going to take credit for the two of you getting together now, I hope you know that."

My boyfriend wraps his arm around my shoulders,

pressing a kiss to my temple. "I'm okay with that," he says. "It means we get to be together."

Twisting in his embrace, I meet him halfway for a kiss and echo his words from the other day. "We'll start our own family."

Sven grins at me. "I can't wait."

epilogue

· · ·

Sven

"ARE you sure you want to do this?" Vanessa looks up at me, her eyes focused on mine. "We don't have to."

"I want to."

She studies me for a moment before she nods. "Okay. I'll support you."

I've written a letter. It was a long, rambling letter: eight pages long, full of heartache and long-repressed emotion. I wrote it by hand, alternating between English and Swedish as I felt the need, pouring out my heart.

And then I shredded it.

There's nothing to gain by sending my parents a fully itemized detailing of all the ways they've disappointed me. Yes, I could try harder to maintain a relationship. But when it's obvious they're not interested, why should I push for it? They call me every six months, if that.

Tucking the card in beside the sonogram picture, I seal the envelope and place an international stamp on it.

We weren't planning on conceiving quite so soon... but we didn't plan on any of this, to be honest. Sometimes it's the things we don't prepare for that teach us the most.

As soon as the test turned up positive, I gave her the ring that had been waiting in my dresser drawer for the last six months, and a few weeks later, we went down to the courthouse to make everything official.

Next month, we're having a party to celebrate the wedding. My parents aren't invited.

And neither are hers.

We've made our own family. Bex and Elsy, Wyatt and Mitch, Robby and Sadie and Arielle and Johanna and Ceci, MacGregor and Jenkins and Jacky...

We don't need loving, doting parents to be the kind of parent our kid will have. We don't need to worry about our terrible relationships with our parents seeping into the next generation.

We've made our peace with our pasts, and we're working diligently to make sure those things don't affect the way we parent.

I wish I understood why parents fail so often.

Mine think I'm silly for playing a game as a career. No matter, only a small percentage of people in the world get to play professional hockey.

Vanessa's have new families and seemingly forget she exists.

Robby's don't approve because of his sexual orientation.

The olive branch I've extended to my parents of simply letting them know they have a grandchild on the way may not change a single thing about our relationship, our dynamic, but I can sleep at night, knowing I've done what I should.

Two weeks ago, just when I thought life couldn't get any sweeter, I lifted the Stanley Cup over my head, surrounded by my teammates and my wife, and the party the book club threw for us overwhelmed me – in a good way.

Showed me that we're bringing a kid into a world where

they'll be loved and supported. A world where anything they can dream, they can achieve.

Even if it takes a second chance at the goal.

———

Want a *spicy* deleted scene about Vanessa and Sven? This shower scene takes place before the epilogue, but after the final scene.

afterword

Thank you for reading *Puck Me Twice*. This book is my baby and I absolutely love it to pieces.

Reviews are more important than readers realize. If you liked this book, please leave me a review!

Join my newsletter to stay in the loop! Lots of unfunny quips, unsuccessful attempts at wit, and general grouching about the writing process.

xoxo,

Allie

what's next?

Thank you for reading Puck Me Twice.

The story continues with *Home for the Holidays*, a Chanukah novella featuring goaltender Jake Lewis and nuclear physicist Rachel, his new roommate… and his brother's ex.

Ready for more hockey? *Body Check* features our fearless captain, Jason McKittrick, and the team physical therapist he can't keep his eyes (or hands) off of…

Want more of the Neurospicy Book Club? Check out *Sportsball is for Lovers*, featuring Sadie and the super hot guy she meets on a kink app… where she learns that six degrees of separation don't always involve Kevin Bacon…

about the author

Allie is a queer and AuDHD writer with a hyper-fixation on inclusivity and representation. She loves the color purple, Michigan football, the Detroit Lions, and the Boston Bruins. When she's not absorbed by a book, she likes to spend time with her nephews.

A San Diego, CA native now residing in South Carolina, she is allergic to the cold, rain, snow, and mosquitos.

also by allie lasky

Meet the Neurospicy Book Club in The Thought of You, where grumpy Johanna finds out she's autistic… because her happy-go-lucky new roomie (and reformed playboy ex-football player) has to tell her.

———

For more Own Voices, try Spark: A Chanukah Novella, where neurodivergent Arielle and her childhood friend Asher finally connect after two decades of missed chances.

———

Want to see how it all started? Read <u>The Game Plan</u> to meet sweet cinnamon roll football player Miles and the feisty sorority girl who stole his heart.